Praise for
JULIA AND THE SHARK:

'A truly beautiful book, with text and illustrations
in perfect harmony. A book to treasure!'
Jacqueline Wilson

'Tom de Freston's stunning illustrations perfectly complement
the poetry of Kiran Millwood Hargrave's story'
Cressida Cowell

'A rich, immersive and wondrous journey,
through deep darkness to hope and light'
Sophie Anderson

'*Julia and the Shark* is deep, beautiful and true. The art shines
and the writing soars. A classic from cover to cover'
Eoin Colfer

'What a gorgeous book – calm, funny, heartfelt, wise,
full of the quiet and force of the sea'
Ross Montgomery

'I fell in love with the tale itself, the setting
(I do love a lighthouse!), the characters and the little details –
it's a beautiful, forceful storm of a book'
Emma Carroll

'There are no wasted words in this book. Like a seashell,
or a flying bird, it is uncluttered and vital. The illustrations,
by Tom de Freston, are mesmerising. I loved it.'
Hilary McKay

'INCREDIBLE. Poignant and lyrical and beautiful,
it's my favourite of Kiran's books so far and that
is saying something. Tom's stunning artwork just brings
it to a whole other level'
Cat Doyle

'Truly extraordinary ... it will redefine what a children's book
can look like, in a way that adults will ooh and ahh over,
and children will love because the story is wonderful and the art
is amazing. It is the kind of book that you will want to have on
your shelves and treasure. I can't wait for the world to
fall in love with *Julia and the Shark*!'
Katherine Webber Tsang

Kiran Millwood Hargrave

LEILA
AND THE
BLUE FOX

with
Tom de Freston

Orion

'With our deepest admiration for our designer Alison Padley,
the 'third author' who brings our worlds to the page - K & T

ORION CHILDREN'S BOOKS

First published in Great Britain in 2022 by Hodder & Stoughton Limited

1 3 5 7 9 10 8 6 4 2

Text copyright © Kiran Millwood Hargrave, 2022
Illustrations copyright © Tom de Freston, 2022

The moral rights of the author and illustrator have been asserted.

A CIP catalogue record for this book
is available from the British Library.

ISBN 978 1 510 11027 4
WTS ISBN 978 1 510 11141 7

Printed and bound in China

The paper and board used in this book
are made from wood from responsible sources.

MIX
Paper from
responsible sources
FSC® C104740

Orion Children's Books
An imprint of
Hachette Children's Group
Part of Hodder & Stoughton
Carmelite House
50 Victoria Embankment
London EC4Y 0DZ

An Hachette UK Company
www.hachette.co.uk

www.hachettechildrens.co.uk

For children forced to leave their homes
and make new ones – we hope you are made welcome
and feel loved.

And for our niblings, who are so cherished:
Tilly, Fred, Leo, Emily, Pippa, Isla,
Ted, Albie and Lily.

BASED ON THE TRUE STORY
OF ANNA, THE ARCTIC FOX
WHO CROSSED A CONTINENT

'We are ALL connected across borders . . .
despite the walls you raise.
Because stories are superheroes, you see,
they can walk through your walls'

- *Elif Shafak, author*

The Inuit call her *tiriganiarjuk*, the little white one, though she is dark grey-blue as the thickest ice, as the rocks she scours for food. The scientists tracking her call her Miso, because it is a sweet but sharp name and they think she has a sweet but sharp face. We call her fox, because that is our word in our language, but she is not just fox, or tiriganiarjuk, or Miso.

She is paws thickly coated to move through the coldest lands. She is ears swivelling, listening for cod moving beneath the channels of snow and ice. She is balance as she climbs the steepest cliffs, rootling for eggs and nestlings. She is yaps, and barks, and teeth, a belly with pointed hunger inside it. She is full of needs she has no names for, and follows them like a magnet toward its true North. She is all these things, and more, and only herself.

ONE

*Look them in the eyes, but don't stare, don't blink too much,
smile, not with teeth, with your eyes, but don't squint.*

Leila repeats Mona's instructions in her head, told to her so
often she can hear the rhythm of her older cousin's words in her
ears, the slight panic in her voice even though she was trying not
to let it show. But the face in the mirror won't do as it's told.
She looks exhausted, and the woman standing at the next sink is
starting to stare, soaping her hands longer than needed.

The smell of the airport soap is too sweet and combines with
the chemical toilet stink to make Leila's tummy churn. She should
have eaten the banana Mona made her take. Her backpack is

heavy, and something hard is digging into the small of her back.

She threw everything in when the security man was done searching it, conscious of the flight guardian waiting for her, of people watching her as they walked past. She already stood out, she knew. There were no other children travelling alone. No other girls with black hair, and light-brown skin. No one else who had been coached by their cousin how to look at the immigration officer.

Leila gives up on her face and straightens her rucksack.

Look them in the eyes. Don't stare.

The soaping woman could do with taking Mona's advice. Leila turns and stares back at her. The woman colours, white cheeks pinkening, and before she can lose her nerve Leila strides out of the bathroom, feeling taller.

It doesn't last more than a couple of steps. She bumps right into the flight guardian, releasing a waft of sugary perfume.

'Whoops-a-daisy,' says the woman, who is tanned, thin and blonde, and called Fiona. Fiona, who is dressed in a pencil skirt so tight her knees knock together and heels that clack on the shiny surface of the airport floor, and who seems to think speaking to a twelve-year-old is the same as talking to a six-year-old. 'All OK? Did you wash your hands?'

Leila doesn't dignify that with a response. Fiona's smile falters. 'All right then.' She pats Leila on the head. 'Ready? This way.'

Leila tries to swallow down the lump in her throat as they approach the signs, written in unfamiliar Norwegian, and below it in cursive, *Immigration*. Fiona steers her past the small queues for *National* and *International* arrivals and *Schengen* and *Domestic*, to a narrow strip pressed against the wall. A tired-eyed man sits behind a desk beneath a sign saying

Other.

Leila is unsurprised to see this word: it is what she has felt since she left her aunt's terraced house in Croydon.

They approach him, the final obstacle in this trip months in the making. He's an underwhelming gatekeeper.

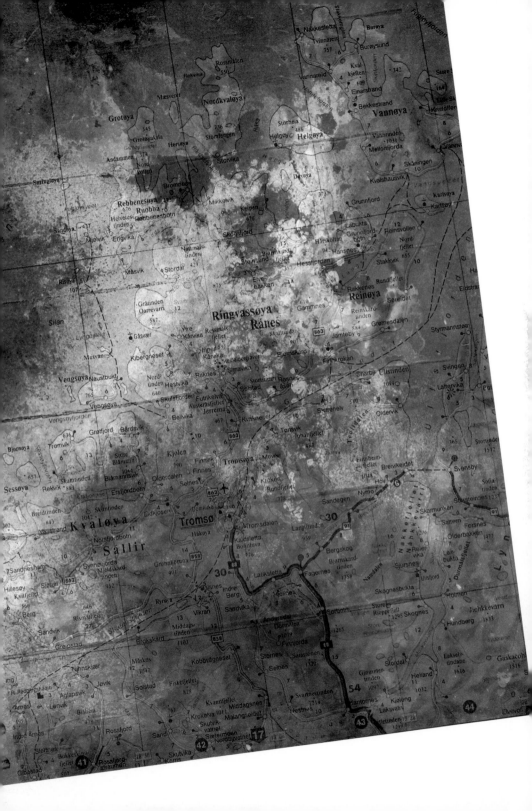

Look them in the eyes, but don't stare, don't blink too much.

The desk is higher than Leila's head. She can just see the top of the man's forehead, where it meets his greying hair. He leans forward a little and holds his hand out to her. Leila fights the absurd urge to shake it.

'Passport,' prompts Fiona, smiling with all her teeth at the immigration officer. Leila curses in her head, imagining Mona's eyes rolling. *Have your passport ready*, she'd said. That's why Leila had gone to the bathroom in the first place, to take some deep breaths and practise her face and make sure her passport was to hand. But the staring woman had thrown her, and now she feels her palms go sweaty as she slings her rucksack off her back to search through it.

Her hand mushes into the banana, gone soft after so long in her bag. She can feel herself smearing it around, over her book and her phone and Mona's earphones, and she's panicking now, trying to remember the last place she'd seen it. Did she leave it in the black plastic tray when the unsmiling man checked her bag?

'Whoops-a-daisy,' laughs Fiona, brandishing the small blue book. 'Forgot you'd given it to me!'

As she hands it over to the officer, Leila fights back tears. *It's all right*, she tells her racing heart. She ducks to zip up her rucksack, wiping her face hurriedly and feeling the sticky banana residue deposit itself on her cheek. Before she can clean it off Fiona pulls her gently back a couple of steps, so the man can compare her photo with her face.

Look them in the eyes, don't stare, don't blink too much. But she is blinking, rapidly, trying to control the tears. She digs her fingernails into her palm as he looks at her. A ball is swelling and swelling in her throat, making it hard to breathe. She hates this, all of it. She hated saying goodbye to Mona and her aunty at the airport, she hated the flight, with its dry, artificial air and Fiona, too silent and too smiley. She hated the man searching her bag, she hated the staring woman and she hates the banana and she hates this man, looking at her like she—

But he's looking down now at her passport. His hand moves in a practised motion, reaching for a stamp, up and down and a satisfying click, then he is handing the passport back, not to Fiona, but to her.

'Welcome to Tromsø,' he says in a lilting, bored voice.

She takes the passport. It was easy, it was over. The part she and Mona had been most scared about. The part she'd had nightmares about, nightmares full of white rooms and bolted down tables. Done. Leila wipes the banana off her face with her sleeve. She feels almost dizzy with relief as she follows Fiona to the conveyer belt, around which bags are already circulating.

'All OK?' asks Fiona. Leila's starting to think it might be.

Leila lets her breath out slowly. It's exhausting being braced all the time, against the staring, the occasional comments. Even at her school, where there are other Middle Eastern girls, even other Syrians. It makes moments like the immigration officer looking away feel like the best sort of relief. If she can't be invisible, she just wants to fit in.

Her bag, a beat-up suitcase borrowed from her aunty, her amma, arrives on its side. Leila stifles a laugh as she watches Fiona in her tight pencil skirt totter against the weight of the suitcase as she manoeuvres it on to its squeaky casters.

'You'll want your coat,' says Fiona. 'Norwegian warmth is less warm than you're used to.'

Leila assumes she means compared to England, which isn't very comforting. She can't remember much of home from before, and Mona won't talk about it. Amma sometimes talks about the markets open to the heat, piled high with fruit she only knows the Arabic names for, about their flat with air conditioning in every room and handwoven rugs they had to leave behind. Basbousa, the cat she and Mum still cry over, left in the care of a neighbour who no longer has regular electricity or hot water. All of these memories have the texture of dreams, fading even as she speaks them.

'Coat!' says Fiona. 'Pop it on.'

Leila unbuckles the belt around the case and unzips the front compartment. Mona packed for her with perfect care, thinking of everything, even rolling her coat with its hood at the top, so Leila can pull it straight out and watch it unfurl like a flag. She slips it on, feeling instantly less conspicuous inside the deep purple jacket, a hand-me-down from Mona of course, but this means it is like new, apart from a rip in the left pocket that Leila sometimes re-rips open when she is especially nervous.

She checks: Mona has stitched it tight shut again. She must be the only seventeen-year-old who still learns sewing. Leila's fingers brush crinkled plastic, and she smiles to herself. Mona has hidden a whole handful of Werther's Originals in there, the gold wrappings like treasure. It's a squeeze of the hand meaning: *you got this.*

'Come along!' says Fiona, too brightly. 'Nearly there!'

She is looking strained, and Leila can tell she wants rid of her. Leila pulls the squeaky-wheeled case after her, and it is only as they approach a final set of automatic doors, she dares think about the main reason her tummy is a string of twisting knots. Because through those doors is the reason for the dozen-page visa application, the face-practising, the trip, all of it. Through those doors, is Mum.

Leila chews her lip as she follows Fiona out into a glass-fronted arrival hall. Her heart has escaped her chest and is pounding somewhere near her ears. She feels hot, her hands clammy, and wonders, too late, if she should have practised her face for this part, too. She scans the unfamiliar crowd. Everyone is white, and tall.

Mum isn't there.

Leila stops walking, but Fiona says, 'there we are,' and click-clacks off towards a white lady in a green puffa jacket, holding a handwritten sign. The sign says **Leila Saleh.** It isn't anyone Leila recognises. Leila feels like she's standing at the top of a cliff, her tummy somersaulting. Mum isn't there. This woman is obviously here to collect her. The disappointment in Leila's chest sharpens quickly into anger.

Six years. Most mums wouldn't be able to wait a moment, a second longer. She knows this because of Amma, because of all her friends' parents clucking at the school gate, beaming as soon as they see their children. They miss them after six hours, let alone six years. But Mum has sent – who? A stranger.

Leila squares her shoulders. Why should she care, if Mum so clearly doesn't? Fiona is waving her over, a little desperately. Leila follows.

TWO

'I'm Liv,' says the woman kindly. Her voice is gently accented, her smile broad, showing crooked front teeth. Leila's voice is caught in her throat, but she summons a weak smile of greeting in return. 'It's nice to meet you, Leila. I'm your mum's friend. We work together. She sent me to see you safe home.'

Leila's tummy jolts again. Home. Her mum's home without her.

'We just have to wait for – ah! There she is!'

Liv starts waving enthusiastically over Leila's shoulder, and Leila turns to see a girl with a thick blonde plait approaching, carrying a holdall over her shoulder.

Liv sweeps the girl into a one-armed hug. '*Jenta mi!* So tall! Was the flight all right?'

'*Ja,*' sighs the girl, wriggling free and giving Leila a rueful smile.

'English, *jenta mi,*' mock-chides Liv. 'You can see we have company.' She grins at Leila, who wants the ground to swallow her up. 'Leila, this is Britt, my daughter.' Liv pinches her daughter's cheek, looking at her with such evident pride it makes Leila feel hollow inside. 'Come from her school in Bergen. A nice friend for you on your visit.'

Leila chances a glance at Britt, who doesn't look horrified at the suggestion of friendship. A bloom of relief grows in Leila.

'Your mum really wanted to be here,' says Liv, already starting to walk towards the exit. Leila opens her mouth to say bye to Fiona, but she's already clacked away. 'We had to apply for emergency funding, and as she's the director she had to be there. But she'll be meeting us for dinner.'

Us? So not only did Mum send a stranger, Leila's now expected to hang out with her and her daughter for hours. Leila grinds her teeth as she follows Liv into the rotating doors leading outside. As soon as she steps into the doors, she feels the chill sucking at her, the glass cold under her fingertips. Fiona was right – the weather here has an extra sharpness to it, the taste of ice hitting the back of your throat.

'Parked just over here,' says Liv, not breaking her stride. 'It's a short drive. We go under the sea! Tromsø is an island, did you know?'

Leila nods, though she didn't know. She hadn't looked up Tromsø online, or read the guidebook Mum sent via Amma, or done anything that might jinx the fact she was going, finally, to see where Mum lived. Where she had left England and Leila for.

Britt has hung back and nudges Leila with an elbow. 'She's a lot, but it's OK. Tromsø isn't so bad, especially in summer.'

Leila's first impressions aren't great. The sky feels lower than normal, pressing down like a hand held flat, and the sun is filtered through cloud so everything feels underwater and dim.

'Here we are,' smiles Liv, unlocking her car and clicking open the boot. Leila's eyes widen as she sees chains – actual *chains* – in the boot. Thick, heavy, medieval looking. Her mind races. Is this a trap? Is she about to be kidnapped?

'Snow chains,' says Britt, who must have noticed Leila's dismay. 'For the tyres.'

Liv shoves them aside with a grunt, and heaves Leila's case in beside them. 'I never remember to take them out, and by the time I do it's time to put them back on!'

'It's early summer, Ma,' sighs Britt. 'If you do it now it'll be months before you need them again.'

'My *lillemor*,' says Liv, ruffling Britt's hair.

'Little mother,' Britt explains, swinging her holdall on top of the chains. 'It's a Norwegian thing.'

'It's a *you* thing,' says Liv, climbing into the driver's seat. 'I've

never known such an old child. I swear she was born reminding me we'd run out of milk.'

'I wouldn't have needed to remind you if you remembered,' says Britt, and Leila feels the atmosphere shift between them.

Leila dithers, feeling shy to open the passenger door, but Britt does it and levers the seat forwards so she can climb into the back, leaving Leila to slide awkwardly into the front seat. In the wing mirror, she can see Britt is staring determinedly out of the window, arms crossed.

'Seatbelts!' says Liv, with a fraction of her former brightness.

Within minutes of leaving the airport the landscape starts to change, and Leila sees snatches of the promised sea that surrounds Tromsø. And then, there, suddenly, is a mountain.

Leila tries not to let her jaw fall open. She has never seen a mountain in real life before. The ones they left behind that surrounded Damascus are so far back in her memory she can't

summon them to the surface any more. The closest she's come to something that height is Box Hill, where she's been orienteering with school. But this is huge, just casually rising and rising and still rising up by the side of the road, so high she can't see the top, dotted with houses and trees that are made special by the fact they are clinging to an actual *mountain*.

She doesn't give away that her heart is starting to pound, and resists the urge to twist in her seat as the car turns and begins to dip into the mouth of a massive tunnel.

'Under the sea we go. Better hold your breath!' says Liv, puffing her cheeks and pursing her lips like a fish. Leila smiles weakly. 'Britt used to love that, didn't you?'

'Used to,' says Britt. As the orange light of the tunnel washes over them, Leila shoots her another glance in the wing mirror. Her arms are still crossed, her brow still furrowed. Leila feels sorry for Liv, who is obviously trying her best with not only her daughter but her friend's daughter.

Then again, Leila knows something about mums being annoying, mums letting you down, mums not showing up when they're meant to and not saying the right thing. So she feels sorry for Britt, too.

The tunnel goes on and on, the journey not helped by the silence. Mona would not like it. She hates small spaces, dark places, anything underground. She takes the bus everywhere, refusing to get on the tube even though it's much faster. Leila doesn't tease her about it, because she knows it's to do with home, Damascus, with the things they don't talk about like hiding and fleeing, and their journey to England, the detention centre. Mona remembers it all, but seems determined to scrub it from her tongue even if she can't do the same for her mind.

Ahead, a speck of light appears, and the road begins to rise, so sharply Leila has the urge to duck like she might hit her head on the top of the tunnel. The speck widens and widens, and they flash out of the tunnel into that flat light, Leila's eyes adjusting.

'Welcome to Tromsø, named after Tromsøya, which is the name of the island we're on,' Liv explains. 'It's the third largest, most northerly city in the world.'

Liv indicates, and the car turns on to a road edging the sea. Forgetting her attempted coolness, Leila twists in her seat. All around them are more mountains. At the very top, before the clouds begin to enclose them, Leila sees snow, lying in white rivulets in the lines of the peaks. It's like a film set.

They drive on in silence, past modern concrete buildings, following the natural curve of the island city, and then ahead of them is a massive bridge formed mostly of thin metal wires, making it look held up by thread. It stretches all the way across an expanse of water, to a cluster of houses settled in the basin at the throat of more mountains, in the middle of which is a building that stands taller than the others, an assemblage of white triangles. It's unlike any structure Leila has seen before, like a set of triangular Russian dolls nested into each other, fronted by a shining pane of glass that reflects the dim light.

'The Arctic Cathedral,' says Liv. 'Isn't it lovely? They have midnight concerts there all summer.'

Leila still can't find her voice. It is lovely. It looks like something from a story, and she wonders what it would look like inside – like standing in a glass snowglobe, with all the snow outside.

Leila stifles a yawn. Her eyes and brain are overloaded by this new place, made heavy by the early start, the bus and the tube to the airport, lugging the case between her and Mona up and down so many steps. And then the adrenaline of the journey itself, heart beating harder every time she had to hand over her passport or walk past a white official, even though there were plenty of faces like hers at the airport. The disappointment and anger of Mum not coming to meet her.

She was tired, bone tired. At that moment, all she needed was her bed.

This place, the place we start and she was born, is rocks and sea. She opened her eyes here when she was a cub, wriggling and burrowing into her brothers and sisters for warmth. She will never be so warm again. Even then, she was all need: scenting up to her mother's belly to feed and later following her father, scavenging with him at the shore.

They have met here, her mother and father fox, on this rocky beach, every year for all their lives, and will do so until one of them dies.

This is another need – one mate for life, finding and losing and
re-finding each other, certain as seasons.

Another reason she walks.

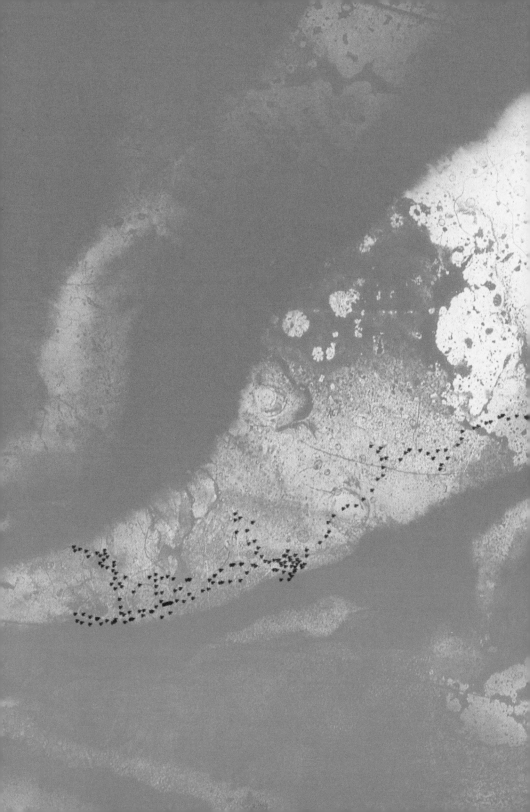

The rocks are jagged and smooth by turns, worked into shapes by tides and storms. She knows the world in shades: danger and safety, hunger and hunt. Can she eat it, might it eat her?

She learns fast because that is how you must, to live. They are lessons learnt not by heart but by claw and teeth, smell and taste.

She walks to the next beach, and back. In the opposite direction she trots, and then back. She grows her world, collecting scents, searching out new safety.

Then it is time and she travels further, across the next beach and the next.

This time, she does not turn back.

She finds a cove,
still rocks and sea,
and rubs her head upon it.
This is how she makes a home.

THREE

Liv is now driving through streets that become more uniform, with rows of neat, square houses.

'The city centre is prettier,' says Liv. 'There are loads of wooden houses, original ones from the first settlers.'

'Not the first,' says Britt. 'The Sámi were here first.'

'The Sámi and the Norse both,' says Liv, nodding. 'Both have settled here for centuries. I meant the men and women who made the city as we know it, as a fishing outpost and trading point. Fish,' she smiles at Leila and draws into an underground parking lot beneath a concrete apartment block, 'are a big deal here. Do you like cod?'

Leila nods, thinking of fish fingers and chips when Mona's left in charge of cooking.

'Excellent,' says Liv, squeezing the car into a narrow spot between two concrete posts and cutting the engine.

The underground light of the car park is a harsh white, making Leila's skin look sallow in the car window. This is another, more silly reason Mona hates being underground – the lighting is unflattering on her skin. 'Sunlight!' is her mantra. 'Sunlight so I shine!'

'OK,' says Liv, opening the passenger door, jolting Leila back into herself. She has a firm hold of Leila's case. 'This way.'

She follows them to a locked door that Liv opens with a key fob, then into a narrow landing in front of a lift. It's all quite high-tech, the lift doors opening smoothly and no stink inside.

The lift opens on to a featureless corridor with doors at either end, grey-blue scratchy carpet and white walls with a single framed photo of misted mountains hanging directly opposite the lift doors.

'Here we are,' says Liv, leading them left and fumbling for her keys. The small plastic sign below the peephole says **Dr Liv Nilsen** in typed black lettering. And – Leila's stomach twists – added in black biro, in Mum's clear hand: **Professor Amani Saleh.**

'You live together?' says Leila.

'Like students!' laughs Liv. 'It's fun.'

The door swings open directly on to a tiny cramped sitting room with two sagging sofas and a low table between them. A cooking area is crammed into the only wall without a door set into it. Leila sees, with a slight feeling of dizzying recognition, Mum's cherished copper ladle, her much used garlic press.

'I guess science doesn't pay so well sometimes,' says Britt, gesturing around the small room. 'Especially when you get obsessed with foxes.'

'Not just any fox,' says Liv, eyes shining with sudden excitement as she wheels the case inside and props it against the wall below a row of hooks. 'We spend most of our time at the institute, so this is really all the space we need. Pop your coat here.'

Leila turns and sees her mum's beige trench coat hanging from a hook, smells the rosewater she washes her face with each morning. Mum had found that coat on a market stall covered in cheap pashminas, had swung Leila around in excitement at such a find.

Leila pushes the memory away. She tugs off her coat and hangs it over the trench coat, hiding it from view. The tiny size of the apartment is another shock. She knows part of the reason Mum left was money – this job being better than anything she'd been offered in the UK. But it seems that was a lie.

'You and Britt will be sleeping here,' says Liv, pointing at the sofas. Leila sees two sets of pillows and duvets folded neatly on the arms. 'It's actually bigger than our bedrooms.'

Liv opens two of the doors set next to each other, and Leila peers around her to see two identical, single beds pushed against the wall and desks set under the windows.

She can tell which one is her mum's because there's the smell of roses and her pink cotton razai on the bed. There is nothing of Leila. Not the pictures she drew in the early days and posted, at great expense to Amma, for birthdays and Eid. Not even a photo of them together.

'This,' says Liv, squeezing past Leila into her room, which has a photo of Britt on the desk, 'is our fox.'

She moves aside a pile of papers and brandishes a large print-out. Leila takes it. It shows a stony beach, backed by larger grey rocks, and edged with a gunmetal grey sea. But there's no fox.

'See her?' grins Liv. Leila shakes her head. But Liv comes to stand behind Leila, and points at a patch of grey stone. 'There.'

Leila squints, holding the paper up closer to her face. She sees, suddenly, a pointed face, a low-slung back, a scrubby tail. It's no wonder she hadn't spotted the fox sooner. It looks nothing like the foxes in London, with their russet fur. This fox blends perfectly with the rocks, with the blue-grey of the sea. It is looking directly at the camera, with an impenetrable gaze.

'We've named her Miso,' says Liv fondly. 'Your mum picked

the name, after the soup at her favourite restaurant. We're going there tonight. Are you hungry?'

Leila shakes her head. She wants desperately to be on her own.

'She's tired, Mamma,' says Britt. 'Shall we go to Smørtorget?'

'Yes!' says Liv delightedly, and Leila glances gratefully at Britt. 'That is,' says Liv, 'if you will be all right?'

'I'm just going to go to sleep,' says Leila. 'I'll be fine on my own.'

Smell of something rotting,

irresistible.

Fox noses toward it,
ears searching for the danger.
Silent.

Under the smell another smell:
more unfamiliar,

strange.

No matter, she follows it.
There, a morsel,
enough to quiet her belly a moment.

Snap
goes the trap.

Fox is in a cage, to her a nameless place with no way out. The strange smell approaches, grows into a shape that walks on two legs like a bear, but smaller. It reaches for her and she is teeth and claw and fight. Her jaws are closed and held stuck, her eyes are covered. Such dark. Her heart, which she trains to beat slow around prey, quickens to a scurry. Around her neck a circle, like the casing of ice after she dives the snow.

Click.

Such light,

    muzzle freed,

        and fox runs

        and runs

            until the cage is behind,

                her cove is behind,

                    the danger is behind.

She checks her belly, sniffs her legs, scuffs in the ground until she smells of herself again. Not hurt, but she carries around her neck that circle, a weight like something lying across it.

It takes some getting used to. She paws at it like a tick, but much like she learnt to walk and hunt and dive and breathe, much like she learnt the growing edges of herself, she is used to it after a while. She finds a new cove, and is careful of easy food.

Weeks pass,

to her they are nameless,

they are fading and growing light,

the warming of weather.

She is still less than a year old when a new need rises, and she
turns her back once more to all she knows.

On this day, she wakes,

and begins to walk.

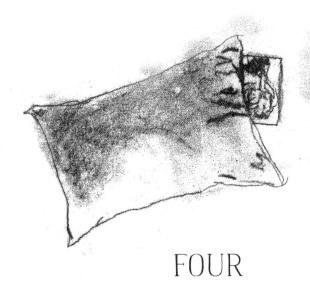

FOUR

Leila lies awake in Mum's narrow bed, staring into the pitch black. Before she left, Liv insisted Leila nap in the bedroom instead of on the sofa, and showed her the control panel that operated the black-out shutters that came down clack-clacking and plunging the room into total darkness. *Essential for the months of midnight sun*, she said, *when it's bright as midday in the middle of the night.*

Leila hasn't ever lain in darkness so deep as this. She can't even use her phone to illuminate it – a brief attempt to switch it on earlier showed the buttons sticky with banana, and even though she didn't know if it would work, she left it in a bag of rice in the kitchen. Hajjar brand, the same as they have at home.

She rolls over. The curtains in her room at home are lined, homemade by Amma, but the streetlamp directly outside always sends in its orange glow. If she reaches further back, she has the impression of a similar sort of light coming through pale-blue cotton blinds, the sort you pull up with a string.

Six years is a long time, and Leila wonders if Mum will be the same as she was in the rare memories Leila allows herself to open, like finding the beige trench coat. Their conversations over FaceTime and WhatsApp are always weirdly formal, always full of people coming and going – Amma and Mona plucking the phone out of Leila's hand and commenting on how pale Mum looks, how she's going grey at the temples, what is she eating there, can she get fresh mangoes?

Her mind feels porous, the memories from before leaking through easier than ever before, and she doesn't like it. For years she's kept them at bay, held them behind her new life – her *only* life – in London, with Mona and Amma, and her friends – blocks bricking over Mum and Damascus. Those blocks feel less solid now, more like a patchwork quilt coming apart at the stitches.

It had been easy, with Mum at a distance, reduced to the size of a phone screen or a photo on the wall. But here, surrounded by her scent, her stuff, Leila feels herself sinking, sucked backwards into quicksand. It is important she struggle, not go down easy.

There is pain there. Anger. Loss. Not things she wanted to feel, that anyone wants to feel.

Leila punches the pillow to get it into a comfier shape, and something crinkles. She shoves her hand blindly under the pillow, and pulls out a square of stiff paper. From its texture, she can tell it's a photograph. Leila gropes for the bedside light, and clicks it on.

It's like a punch to the gut. It's a photo of them together, the one Amma has a copy of, taken on the rooftop of their apartment block in Syria, the light that golden colour Mona says suits her skin best. Leila three years old and on Mum's shoulders, both of them with their heads thrown back and laughing.

Leila sits up, holding the photo. Mum had this under her pillow, like something precious, like something she'd want to dream about. Tears prickle Leila's lids, and she wipes them away roughly with her pyjama top. She is still angry. But perhaps Mum had missed her, after all.

FIVE

The restaurant is hot and crowded, the windows cloudy with condensation. Customers sit side by side on long benches with joint tables and eat from large steaming bowls. Everyone seems to be talking at once, in Norwegian and English, but all of it fades out when Leila sees Mum.

She's sitting in the back corner of the restaurant, talking to a waiter. They're both laughing at something, and Leila sees her as a stranger might. Her hair is the same neat, straight black bob, her lipstick red as ever. She's dressed all in black, like a spy or a movie star. Her eyeliner flicks are neat as Mona's.

'Woah,' breathes Britt. 'Is that your mum? She's so pretty.'

It's obvious it is her mum, because again, everyone is white apart from the Japanese waiter, who is now writing something down on his pad. Mum looks absently around, and finally notices them, standing at the doorway.

Leila shrinks down into her coat, even though she's already starting to sweat in the heat of the restaurant. She wishes they weren't doing this here, now. She isn't ready.

But Mum is standing up, holding out her arms, and Leila walks into them, biting her tongue hard to keep from crying. Waves crash in her chest, rocking her bodily. All the anger fades for a moment and there is only this: it feels so good to be held by her mother.

Mum is shorter, or rather Leila is taller, able to rest her head on Mum's shoulder. She breathes her in, and Mum holds her tightly and whispers into the top of her head, 'Leila.'

Leila draws back. 'Hi Mum,' she says, more coldly than she feels. Mum is looking at her with bright eyes, and Leila sits down on the seat opposite her, thumping down hard on the wooden bench, and sliding along to make room for Britt.

'You must be Britt,' smiles Mum, turning her light beam on to Liv's daughter. 'Heard so much about you.'

Her accent is smoother, not vanished completely but folded into something else, like cake batter on its way to becoming combined. Liv hangs up the coats while Mum flaps, jabbering

about jasmine tea, her hands fluttering like golden brown wings.

She's nervous, thinks Leila, *as nervous as me. More, maybe. Good.*

The waiter puts steaming cups in front of them, and Mum slurps noisily.

'Here we are,' she says, laying her palms flat on the table-top. 'At last. I so wanted to meet you at the airport, La-La.' Leila flinches at the nickname. 'I'm sure Liv explained. There's been an issue with funding and . . . but it's all sorted now.'

'All sorted?' says Liv jovially, plonking herself next to Mum. 'We got it?'

'We got it!' says Mum, and the two women high-five. Leila feels Britt shudder with embarrassment. 'This will change everything.'

Leila looks down. She doesn't understand what they're talking about any more than she recognises anything on the menu.

'Shall I order for you, La-La?' asks Mum. 'Do you still like prawns?'

'No,' says Leila sharply, though she does. She orders something called *tori-katsu* because she can pronounce it.

'Good choice,' says Mum encouragingly, 'How was your flight?'

'Fine.'

'No trouble at the counters?'

'Counters?' says Liv.

'Immigration,' says Mum. 'She still has her Syrian passport.'

'You're Syrian?' says Britt.

'Yeah,' says Leila hotly. 'So?'

'Just your accent,' says Britt, holding up her hands in mock surrender. 'You sound like you're from London.'

'Born in Damascus,' says Mum. 'We came when she was five.'

'I don't remember it,' lies Leila. 'Just London.'

Mum looks at her and Leila deliberately avoids her gaze. 'How's Mona?'

'She's fine. You talked to her last week.'

'My niece,' says Mum to Britt. 'Seventeen. She just passed her driving test.'

'Three months ago,' says Leila.

'La-La—'

'Leila.'

'Leila.' Mum's hand reaches for hers and she shoves them on to her lap. The anger is back, sharp and hotter even than this overcrowded restaurant. 'Please. Let's not— Don't—'

'What?' hisses Leila, even though she hates making a scene. Mum falls silent, her hand retracting.

'Your funding,' says Britt into the awkward silence. 'Mamma explained a little, but she wasn't sure if you'd get it.'

'Yes,' says Mum, swallowing hard. 'Yes. It's amazing news. Life-changing, really. This fox, an Arctic fox we've been following for a while now. We managed to get a tracker collar on her in winter.'

'That can't have been easy,' says Britt. Liv and Mum laugh, and Leila folds harder into herself, feeling outside it all.

'It wasn't,' says Liv. 'She's smart, is Miso. But Dr Saleh is smarter.'

Mum waves her hands dismissively. 'Rotten reindeer meat and a trap isn't so smart. Just lucky she was hungry enough when passing.'

'Right on cue!' says Liv, as the waiter returns, setting down four black cups. 'Thanks Tim. Miso soup!'

Leila peers uncertainly down. It's a cloudy liquid with green stuff floating in it, like pond water.

'So why did you need more funding?' asks Britt, slurping. 'If you already fitted the tracker?'

Leila hates Britt a little, how informed she seems, how confident she is asking questions about this research Mum has never talked about. Even though her work was clearly more important to her than being a mum. Leila sips the soup to hide her expression, and is surprised to find it tastes good, salty and rich, like broth.

'Because that was only the start,' says Mum. 'About a month ago, we noticed she was on the move. She was born in a litter of cubs on a beach in Svalbard, near our research centre there. It's usual for them to scatter a bit, but Miso has been walking for weeks now, across the sea ice, miles at a time, going north and then west. Obviously the weather is doing weird things at the moment,' Mum sips her soup. 'The Gulf Stream is showing signs of shifting, we're seeing colder and hotter cycles than ever. It's not looking great.'

'No doom and gloom,' says Liv. 'Not today. Today we are celebrating.'

'Yes,' says Mum. 'Because Miso has walked nearly a thousand miles in a month. A month! It's further than any fox I've tracked before.'

'She's showing us a new shape to the world,' interjects Liv. 'She's proving animals can adapt through migration even in these most extreme times.'

'Just like people,' says Mum, and Leila feels her eyes on her again.

'So, with this funding,' says Liv. 'We can follow her.'

Britt chokes a little on her soup, and Leila takes a bit too much pleasure slapping her on the back. 'You're going across the sea ice too?'

'In parts,' says Liv. 'Mostly by boat.'

'Why don't you fly?' says Britt. 'There are sea planes, aren't there?'

Liv opens her mouth, but Leila thinks she sees a warning glance pass from Mum to Liv, and the woman clears her throat.

'Too expensive. We can track her from here of course, but

it's not the same as being there on the ground, observing her interactions with other animals, seeing whether her coat changes colour or her eating habits change.'

Tim, the waiter, returns and takes their empty soup bowls, then sets down rectangular boxes in front of them. Leila is relieved to see she recognises everything on hers: rice, dumplings, salad and breaded chicken. Tim even brings cutlery without her asking so she can cut it all up.

Mum has some sort of silvery fish on top of her rice. She sees Leila looking and snaps her chopsticks together. '*Unagi*. Eel. Want some?'

Leila wrinkles her nose. She didn't even know you could eat eel. She certainly never guessed her mum would. Maybe she was like the fox, its eating habits changing the longer it spent further north.

'So, when are you going?' asks Britt, who ordered sushi in rainbow colours. Liv and Mum look at each other. Mum sets her chopsticks back down on their little china rest.

'Well,' she says. 'That's sort of up to you.'

'Me?' says Britt.

'You, and La–. . . Leila.'

The rice goes extra sticky in Leila's throat. Was Mum about to send Leila straight back to London? After it took so much to get here.

'The question is, do you want to come too?' says Mum. It's addressed to them both, but she's looking right at Leila.

'To Svalbard?' says Britt, her voice incredulous. 'With the polar bears and the whales and all of it? For real?'

'For real,' says Liv. 'But further north than Svalbard, now. Greenland, at this rate.'

Britt whoops quietly. 'Yes! Oh wow. I mean,' she seems to remember herself and shrugs coolly. 'Sure.'

Leila's insides are churning. A boat. Following a fox in the Arctic Circle. And she thought Tromsø was enough of an adventure. She's half thrilled, half terrified at the idea. She's never been on a proper boat, only on the river bus.

'You want me to come with you?' she asks Mum, and this time when Mum reaches across the table and takes her hand, Leila doesn't pull away.

'Yes.'

Leila smiles. The waves in her chest swell again. 'All right then.'

The
ground is
different
from what
she is used to.
No rocks here,

only ice.

She loses the scents of things more easily, and goes longer without food. The last of the winter dark empties from the sky. It is the first summer she has had her eyes open, the first summer she's walked alone.

The skies fill with birds, too high for her to reach. She is far from the nesting grounds, from puffins and terns, and other easy meals. The hunger starts to be constant, sucking at her belly like a parasite. She knows better than to turn back, to retrace ground that has not fed her. She can only go on, now.

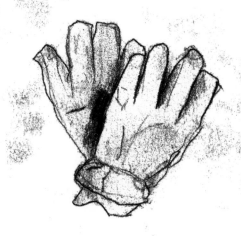

SIX

'How come your mum loves Arctic foxes so much?' whispers Britt into the darkness between the sofas. Leila lies with her eyes stretched wide open, trying to drink in any light at all, but there is none. The black-out blinds are doing their job well, because after they walked back from the restaurant it was still as light as though it were the afternoon.

'I didn't know she did,' whispers Leila. 'She's a meteorologist. I thought she was here to study weather patterns. What about your mum?'

'She likes everything,' says Britt on a sigh. 'It was polar bears first, then orcas, now foxes. She moves around so much no one will give her funding. Your mum must be good at her job, to get this boat sorted.'

'Yeah,' says Leila again.

'You haven't seen her for ages, right?' says Britt. Leila feels her cheeks flush, but it's easier to talk in this blackness.

'Six years.'

'Six *years*?' Britt lets out a low whistle.

'Yeah. We talk on the phone and stuff,' says Leila, feeling weirdly defensive.

'Why'd she come here?'

'I don't know,' says Leila, but she does, a bit. She heard Amma fighting with Mum about it on the phone, hears Mona and her aunt discussing it when she's meant to be in bed. The job is one thing, of course. But it's also because it's as far away from home as she can be. Because everything is different, from the food to the clothes to the weather, because she doesn't want to remember home. And really, though no one says it, because she doesn't want to remember Leila.

'And you live with your aunt and cousin?'

'Good memory,' says Leila, shifting uncomfortably. She's not used to people paying her this much attention.

'My friends think it's strange I only spend summers with Mamma,' says Britt, 'But I don't mind really.'

'Where are you the rest of the time?' asks Leila, grateful to have a change of subject.

'Bergen, with Papa,' says Britt on a yawn. 'And Sanna, his wife, and Laurie and Jenna, my half sisters. They're six and two.'

Leila braces herself for Britt to ask about her father, but she doesn't. Instead she keeps talking, her voice becoming sleepier.

'Mamma is strange, like her brain is always moving on. A bit like that fox, I guess. It suits us, me coming in summer. But that doesn't mean I don't miss her, you know? I'm just telling you this, because I think you might understand. Better than my friends in Bergen do. That sort of double life, or half life, whichever way you want to look at it.'

Leila feels a tingling in her chest, something opening that had been held tight shut, a fist releasing. Everything Britt said made sense. She did understand. And so maybe Britt would understand her too.

'Britt?' she says softly, but she can tell by the girl's breathing she is already asleep. Leila wriggles into a comfier position. In two days, they would be on a boat to places she'd never heard of. And even if Mum was driving her mad, she would be with Britt. She wouldn't be alone.

There are a lot of preparations to be made for travelling north. Leila needed snowshoes and walking poles, goggles and gloves that made her hands double in size. She stood in the smelly boot room of the research institute, where they were borrowing all their equipment from, flexing her hands like Iron Man.

Mum starts unhooking snow goggles from the railing where they're hung up like discarded pelts. 'Blue or yellow?'

Leila leans in and gives them a sniff. She'd chosen the gloves based on how little they smelt like old sweat and metal. 'Blue.'

'Like our little fox!' smiles Mum. Leila turns away, pretending to study the walking poles: light, shiny sticks in neon colours with sharp spikes at one end.

This is the first time she's been alone with Mum since she arrived. She'd been excited, secretly, to see where Mum worked, to see this place that kept her from London and Leila. They'd taken a bus that had looped further out of the city, up a hillside planted with colourful flowers, to a large concrete and glass building with a sign:

TROMSØ ARCTIC INSTITUTE

Once inside, they'd walked long corridors that looked and smelt like a school, Mum waving to pretty much everyone inside and introducing Leila to Dr this and Professor that. It was impossible to miss the looks of surprise as the tall, mostly male, all white strangers smiled at her or awkwardly shook her hand in the manner of all adults who don't know what to do when faced with children. Had Mum not told anyone about her?

Mum had shown Leila her office, which she shared with Liv and a junior researcher called Matty, who would also be coming on the boat. Like the flat, it had a cramped, lived-in feel, the computer screens blocky and the keyboards with keys crunchy and cubed as blocks of toffee.

'A miracle worker, your mother,' smiled Matty, who Mona would have called cute. He had glasses and a square jaw. 'How she wrangled so much cash!'

'It was all in your application,' said Mum, waving away his admiration. 'Besides, who could resist the chance to get closer to Miso?'

She grinned stupidly at the walls, papered with photographs of the fox, walking across the same featureless landscape. A map filled the main wall, showing the top portion of the world, curved off by a line labelled 'The Arctic Circle'. It took Leila a moment to recognise it at all, so used was she to seeing maps of the whole world, Europe at the centre and the rest unfolding from it. But of course, the world didn't have a centre like that, not really. It was all to do with who drew the map, and what they thought was important. This map was clearly made by people who thought nothing was more thrilling that this expanse of white and water.

'We are here,' said Mum, landing her finger on a speck labelled 'Tromsø'. 'And Svalbard is here.' She moved her finger almost halfway up the map, to a large mass of islands. It was much bigger than Leila expected it to be. There was a thread attached to a blue-topped drawing pin at the western coast.

'That's where she was born,' said Mum, in a hushed tone, like she was in a library. 'And this is where she lived, before she started her journey.' Mum traced the thread to another pin an inch from the first. 'And this is where she has walked.' Mum chased the thread up and up. 'On to the Arctic Sea. One thousand and sixty miles, so far.'

'One thousand, one hundred miles,' said Matty cheerfully. 'Latest reading's just in.'

'Let me see!' cried Mum excitedly, shouldering past Leila and peering at the computer screen. She was following the fox anywhere it led, when she hadn't even come to find Leila, even though she knew exactly where she was. Leila turned back to the map. She traced the thread, imagining that tiny fox in this huge expanse, walking alone. Why was it doing this? And what if the sea ice ran out?

In the boot room, Mum holds poles up against Leila's hip. 'They are adjustable, but still. This one looks a good height.'

Leila takes the pole awkwardly. She can barely feel it through the thick gloves. Mum claps her hands.

'You look marvellous! A regular Amundsen. Polar explorer,' she says at Leila's raised eyebrow. 'Come on, you must know him?' She tuts. 'The British school system is so biased. I expect you'll have learnt all about Captain Scott?'

Leila feels a bubbling in her belly. 'No.'

'Scott of the Antarctic? Really, La-La—'

Leila throws down the stick and yanks off the gloves. Her palms are sweaty, her face hot, her stomach churning. 'Don't call me that! No one calls me that any more, which you'd know if you'd been around instead of here, naming foxes—'

'Leila—'

'And no, I don't know who Almond's son is, or Scott, or you in fact. I don't know who you are at all, but I guess we're even, because you obviously don't know who I am, either!'

Mum reaches out to her, but she jerks back, knocking the walking poles sideways and setting off a chain reaction, sending them clattering like dominoes. She tugs open the door and tumbles outside into the bracing pale day, trampling through flowerbeds and high grasses, all of it a blur, eyes stinging in the cold.

She draws up just short of a steep drop. In front of her is

the sea, stretching on and on. She balls her fists, shoves them under her armpits, but still her skin tingles and crawls with the cold. The air here is sweet and clean as bottled water, and she gulps it down, feeling her tears drying coldly on her cheeks. The sea and the sky melt and blend, colours running into each other.

'Leila?'

She doesn't know how long she's been standing there. Long enough for the cold to leach through her jumper and make her shiver. She feels Mum drop her coat over her shoulders, and lets her guide her gently backwards, until she feels a stone wall behind her knees. She sits down with a heavy thump, and Mum slides up next to her.

'I'm sorry,' says Leila, to break the silence.

'You don't need to apologise. I do,' says Mum, but the word *sorry* doesn't actually leave her mouth. 'We don't have to go. We can send Liv, and Matty, and you and I can stay here in Tromsø, or drive south a bit. Anything you want.'

Leila wants to shout, *I don't know what I want.* Instead, she shakes her head. 'It's OK.'

'You're sure?'

Leila isn't sure. But she doesn't want to have to make a decision. She doesn't want to have to think at all. Mum puts her arm around her and pulls her in close.

'It's beautiful, the Arctic. It's like being in another world, or outer space.'

This is already another world, thinks Leila. *Me and you together.* The smell of Mum's rosewater is almost overwhelming, and Leila has to bite down hard on her tongue to stop the tears reappearing. She hates her, and she loves her. She doesn't want to be here, and is already dreading having to leave. It's like what Britt was saying, about the half life, or double. While Mum was away, it was easy to swell her life in London to fill the gaps she'd left. But now Leila is here with her, feeling her warmth and hearing her laugh, the absence feels sharper, ragged. Being with her has made all that time without her far more painful.

Leila forces herself to pull away, looking at the trampled flowers.

'I didn't mean to wreck them.'

'We'll put it right,' says Mum, and Leila hopes she isn't only talking about the flowerbeds.

SEVEN

It is so early Leila feels nauseous when Mum shakes her gently awake. She opens the electronic blinds a crack, and the light pours in as though it's midday, not three in the morning.

They huddle in their coats, Britt and Liv pale as blank paper, and take turns lugging their assorted bags, snow gear, and a large wire cage in case they need to catch Miso, in the lift to the ground floor foyer.

'We don't use this exit at all in winter,' says Liv, yawning widely. 'The snow heaps up higher than the door.'

Leila shudders. She doesn't understand how Mum lives like this. Mum, who always tilted her head to catch the last of the sun, who loved long walks and bright colours (where were these memories coming from, like a sea wall breached, it was dizzying), how she stays shut up in these beige concrete boxes for months at a time, with no sunlight or fresh air. Even now, she's edged close to the window, standing in a square of lemon coloured light, bags heaped around her.

The sight triggers another memory, of Mum surrounded by suitcases and bags, crying because they were leaving their house, their country, but most of all because they were leaving Basbousa, the purring, plump cat who is still alive, still living with their neighbour, among the last in their district of Damascus.

'Here we are!' cries Liv.

There's a taxi outside. Mum springs to instant action, looping her arms through multiple bags and struggling to open the door. Leila hurries forwards and opens it for her.

Leila and Britt hover sleepily as the adults jigsaw their rucksacks, camera bags, Mum's inexplicable tote full of papers, cage and extra coats into the boot, before they all pile into the passenger seats. As the car pulls away Britt goes immediately back to sleep, and Liv and Mum fall to chattering in Norwegian with the taxi driver. Leila has never heard Mum speak it before, and it feels wrong somehow, to hear her voice saying words Leila can't understand.

The inside of the taxi is heated to a sauna. Sweat beads on Leila's forehead and upper lip. Luckily, the roads to the harbour are clear this early in the morning, though Leila sees people out jogging in long leggings on the gritted pavements.

'Summer legs,' says Liv, switching to English. 'The restlessness that comes with the midnight sun. It's always the same this time of year. They'll be used to it by August.'

'Strange, isn't it?' says Mum, nudging her gently, rustling the bags on their laps. Leila knows Mum's talking about the sunlight, but it's all strange. Being here, with her, on an island in the Arctic Circle, bound for a boat that will take them even further north, to follow a fox. Leila imagines Mona's eyebrow arching. She should have texted her by now. Putting her phone in the bag of rice hadn't worked, but she could have messaged from Mum's, or asked to borrow Britt's. It was too early in the morning to do either, now.

'Yeah,' says Leila. 'Very.'

The strangeness only increases when they see their boat. It looks like a locked box, sitting low in the water, painted blue and white and splattered by gulls that are circling and screaming above it, Leila can just make out its name on the side, in flaking paint: *The Floe*.

'It's perfect!' squeals Liv, piling out of the taxi and nearly tripping on a rope as thick as her arm.

Mum clambers out, beaming, and Leila feels cold air pouring into the car. Britt sighs deeply, still sleeping. Leila fumbles in her pocket, and pulls out a Werther's.

In case of emergency, Mona had said. Leila looks at the boat and untwists the golden plastic.

The sweet has shrunk to a sliver by the time Leila sets foot on the boat. They stood around, stamping their feet while the luggage was loaded, and Liv chattered to every member of the five-strong crew like they were old friends.

Mum is a little more reserved than Liv, but it's not like she's shy. She has this air of authority, like a headteacher, that Leila doesn't remember from before. She reapplied her lipstick before meeting the captain, a man with a grey, neatly trimmed beard and sunburnt forehead. Captain Johansson blinks quite rapidly at Mum when she is introduced.

'I hope you are not so much trouble as my last lady scientist,' he says gruffly.

'We're all trouble,' says Mum. She doesn't fit with many people's vision of a scientist, that much is clear. But when she crosses the short mesh gangplank to the boat, there can't be a doubt in anyone's mind that she belongs there.

Leila follows Britt on to the boat. Through the wire floor of the gangplank the sea is grey, foaming softly against the blue hull. Leila feels sick, so she fixes her eyes ahead, past the smiling crew member offering a hand, and tries to imitate Mum's ease.

The boat smells: this is the first thing that hits Leila. Fish, and oil. This must be why there are so many gulls, massing and swirling overhead, searching for an easy meal. The second thing is the certainty they are no longer on solid ground. Something taps at the back of Leila's mind – a memory, knowledge she wants to forget.

The deck is coated in some sort of white grippy paint, but still Leila clutches on to the handrail as she walks around to the front of the boat, where Liv and Mum are standing with their arms around each other, looking out at the sea.

'What do you think?' says Mum, noticing Britt and Leila approaching and turning to smile over her shoulder.

Britt shrugs. 'It's no cruise liner.'

'It's better,' says Mum. 'I'd love to see a liner deal with the ice we're going to face. What do you think, Leila?'

'Yeah,' says Leila. 'It's fine.'

Mum's face crumples a little, and Leila feels an uncontrollable need to make her smile. 'It's good,' she says. 'Smells a bit, but really good.'

'It's a working fishing boat usually,' says Mum, 'but they've done some research trips before. Look here, at the hull.'

She draws Leila up beside her, into the narrow space where the boat funnels into a point. The edge comes up to Leila's chest, and Mum motions for her to put her foot on a metal post. Leila feels a little nervous to raise herself up higher, but she doesn't want to seem cowardly. She steps up, and Mum puts her arm around her.

'Lean over. I've got you. You see?'

She points down into the gunmetal water. Leila can make out the hull beneath the waves, coated in a shiny layer.

'It's not an ice breaker, of course,' says Mum. 'Those are huge. And slow. But this will make any thinner passages of ice easier to deal with. When we get close to shore, this will help us get right in, depending on where Miso decides to lead us.'

'Where is she now?'

'Here,' says Mum, pulling out a creased map, a smaller version of the one on her office wall, the fox's route marked out in red pen. 'Well on her way to Greenland. It'll take us a couple of days to even get close to her vicinity, so we have to anticipate where she might go.'

'If she behaves as she has,' says Matty. 'Following the thickest ice, we expect her to continue west. But she could go north.'

'If she goes too far north, we can't follow,' Mum sighs. 'We have skis and supplies enough for only a few days on the ice.'

'Do you ski, Leila?'

'Of course she doesn't,' says Mum.

Leila flushes.

'Well maybe we won't have to ski,' says Matty. 'Maybe it will all play into our hands.'

Mum spits to ward off the evil eye, and Leila mimics her as a reflex. A horn sounds loudly behind them, and Leila jumps.

The engine starts, a rumbling that vibrates through Leila's soles. Goosebumps shoot up her arms. Mum's hand tightens around her.

'We're going!'

Slowly, so slowly it takes a moment for Leila to register it as movement at all, the boat begins to slide from the harbour. Ahead, the surrounding mountains are wreathed in early morning fog, the light stronger, strengthened to gold.

'You want to stay up here for now, Leila?' says Mum, 'Or go to bed? I think that's where Liv and Britt are.'

'Stay here,' says Leila, and Mum smiles. Her hair is swept back from her face by the sharp breeze, her brown skin shining. Leila's own skin feels rubbed raw by the cold, but she doesn't want to go, doesn't want to break the contact with Mum, break the easy silence that falls between them.

It feels, already, impossibly wild. As the boat begins to pick up speed, Leila has the sense of the world's hugeness. She's never really thought about it before. The journey from Damascus feels abstract, obscured by time, the detention centre like a full stop at the end, casting a long shadow. But now, looking at the endless water, her head feels weightless, like it might lift off her neck and float away.

Leila looks over her shoulder at Tromsø,
the bridge and the magical glass cathedral,
watching the harbour fade from sight behind
them, the sea open out like a book in front.
Leila feels, for the first time, the tingly
beginnings of excitement
in her stomach.

Mona will never believe this.

Sleeping in the light is harder. There are things she can see in the dark better than they can see her, but in this light it is impossible. She has lost her advantage, feels more hunted than ever.

She runs through unchanging, scentless places, though she has
eaten nothing but a mouthful of rotted, scavenged walrus for
days. The ice is thinner. She is thinner, her ribs struck out against
her fur. She is used to the gnawing now. She moves to find thicker
ice, loops a place where she smells a carcass, a whale dead and
floating in the sea, too far to reach.

Around her, the season has changed. Further south, there is moss unfreezing, the buds of flowers forcing through.

For Fox,

there is only the hunger,

and it drives her on through the spring.

EIGHT

Leila's euphoria doesn't last. Soon enough, the boat picks up speed and nausea starts in her belly. She must look pale because Mum rubs her back.

'You tired?'

Leila nods, because she's embarrassed to admit that maybe she's seasick. Mum yawns, her lipstick making her mouth look like a cavern. Leila sees she still has the gap in her molars she remembers from home – Damascus – and with another tug in her stomach she is lying on the floor of their flat, Mum's face blowing raspberries above her, and Leila hooks her small finger through the gap, and Mum whistles through it.

'Come on.'

Mum takes her hand and leads her back around the side of the boat, heaving open a heavy metal door. A waft of closed-off spaces rises to greet them. A steep, narrow staircase disappears down, and the only light comes from feeble bulbs set at intervals in the walls. The door bangs loudly shut behind them. Inside is dark as a pit after the brightness of the endless sun. She follows Mum down the clanging metal steps, until they must be below water.

Down here, the rocking of the boat is more pronounced, and Leila prays that she won't throw up in the tiny toilet that Mum shows her as they walk past.

'It's also the shower,' says Mum, pointing up at the ceiling. 'You just put the seat down, to avoid flooding the toilet.'

Leila swallows down bile. Mona would not tolerate this, any of it. Not the darkness, and definitely not the toilet/shower monstrosity. Mum seems to be seeing a different picture entirely, proudly talking about salt-water filtration and cyclical systems like she's in a five-star hotel showing off a jacuzzi.

'And we're in here,' she says with a flourish, gesturing to a room where Liv's voice is booming from. Leila peers inside. It looks like a prison cell, with four metal bunks set across from each other. Between them is a narrow patch of space that Liv seems to fill entirely. The light here is fluorescent, throwing everything into contrasts of dark and bright.

Leila's vision flickers. That light – she's seen it before, in the detention centre. No light switches, so they woke up when the wardens turned them on, spent evenings in darkness. She'd pile into Mum's single bed, Mona and Amma squeezed into one across from them, trying to ignore the crying of their other roommates while Mum told her stories of magical lands filled with dragons and adventure.

'What's wrong?' frowns Mum. She searches for something to say.

'Where are the bags?' asks Leila faintly.

'Here!' says Liv, grinning. She reaches down and slides open a massive drawer under the bottom bunk, kneeling on the bed to open it fully. Leila sees their rucksacks laid out side by side in there like corpses. 'Just clothes. Everything else is in the corridor storage racks.'

'The luxury,' says Britt from one of the top bunks.

Mum smiles at Leila, 'We'll wake you for some breakfast in a couple of hours. Take your pick of beds!'

She closes the door, leaving them in the stark light.

Leila unlaces her boots and takes off her coat then heaves herself up on to the ladder fixed between the bunks, slithering on to the bed, bending low so as not to hit her head. The ceiling is close enough for her to place her whole palm flat on it.

'Like I said,' says Britt. 'Luxury.' She sighs deeply. 'Papa will be in the Lofoten Islands now.'

Leila snorts. 'Where are the loften Islands?'

'Lofoten,' corrects Britt. 'It's where we all used to go, when they were together. Mamma and Papa. Islands further south. In summer they're so green, and the water is just warm enough to swim in. Papa's family have a cabin there. It's basic, but nothing like this.' She sighs again, and rolls on to her side.

'I'm sorry,' says Leila, not knowing what to say.

'Not your fault. Where's your dad?'

'Not around.'

'Is he still in Syria?'

'Probably.'

'Sorry,' says Britt. 'Being nosy.'

'It's OK,' says Leila. 'He was never around.'

'What was it like, leaving Damascus?'

Leila looks at her sharply.

'Sorry,' says Britt. 'I never know when to stop talking, Papa says.'

'I don't remember anyway.'

Thankfully, Britt doesn't push it. Instead, she yawns and turns off the light. The boat rocks gently. The memory, the knowledge Leila felt when she first stepped on board, taps again, insistent. *No.* Leila tells it firmly. She closes her eyes, and refuses to dream.

*

It's the worst sort of nap, the sort that you wake from thick-tongued and groggy. Leila lies stunned for a few moments after Mum wakes her. She'd forgotten, in the oblivion of sleep, to feel sick, but now she feels her tummy churn again.

'Bit of a rough patch,' says Mum. 'Come up on deck and eat, it'll help.'

Leila slides out of the bunk and into her boots, holding on tightly to the ladder to keep from overbalancing. Mum stops her at the doorway.

'Lace up,' she says. 'No trip hazards on deck.'

Leila rolls her eyes and bends to tie them. When she straightens, Mum is looking at her strangely.

'What?'

'That eye roll,' she smiles. 'You learnt that from me.'

Leila bites back that she learnt it from Mona as Mum leads the way up the stairs, and heaves the door open. Light floods in, and clean, fresh air laced with salt. Leila breathes it deeply in, before a roll of the boat tilts her out the door.

'Steady,' says Mum, and helps right her. 'See what I mean about trip hazards?'

All around them is sea, in every direction. It's like being in a dreamscape, a few string clouds combed overhead, the boat bobbing up and down, the sound of the wind. A totally different world.

The deck is full – all the crew members leaning over the back of the boat, and up front the Captain, Liv and Britt are crowded around a metal box marked LIFEJACKETS. Spread over it is a piece of plastic scattered with pastries and a bunch of unripe bananas.

'Don't get used to this,' smiles Captain Johansson. 'Nothing fresh after the first week. But I do a mean line in spam fritters.'

Britt wrinkles her nose, and Liv laughs. 'There'll be fish, of course. Don't worry.'

Leila forces herself to smile, selecting a circular pastry and taking a bite.

'Ugh!' She spits over the side of the boat. 'Sorry.' She flushes. Amma would never forgive her for spitting food in public.

'I was surprised when I saw you pick that up,' says Mum. 'She always used to pick all the currants out of her Om Ali.'

'What's that?' asks Britt.

'A dessert. I used to make it all the time—'

Mum breaks off suddenly, noticing Leila's expression. Leila knows she is letting her feelings show, but she can't help it.

'Anyway,' says Mum, breezily. 'Have a chocolate croissant?'

She points it out and they eat in silence, looking out over the vast expanse.

The motion of the sea starts to even out, so Leila doesn't feel like she has to cling on to the railing. The pastry clumps and sticks in Leila's throat, and she picks up one of the chilled plastic bottles of orange juice. It tastes like long train journeys and first days of school.

Liv stretches widely. 'Who cares to join me in some digestive aid?'

Britt chokes on her orange juice. 'Mamma. No.'

'Britt, yes,' says Liv buoyantly. She is clearly a morning person. 'Look there's a perfect spot at the rear behind the wheelhouse. All of us could fit!'

Britt rolls her eyes and mutters. 'I'm going back to bed.'

Britt pushes off the railing and disappears back downstairs. Liv's face falls, but she recovers herself quickly and turns beaming to Matty, Mum and Leila. 'How about it?'

'Sure,' shrugs Matty, and Mum nods.

Leila hesitates. 'What is digestive aid?'

'Yoga!' laughs Liv. 'You can do yoga for anything and everything, including getting that breakfast down safely. Nothing worse than toilet issues, except toilet issues on a boat.'

Captain Johansson flushes. 'I better be . . .'

He doesn't even bother finishing his excuse, striding hurriedly to his cabin.

'No mats of course,' says Liv, her breath making little puffs. 'But we have thick socks on. Boots off, all!'

NINE

The crew look on amusedly as Liv arranges them in a staggered line, placing herself slightly in front. Leila shuffles, feeling supremely self-conscious. Liv plants her feet apart and says, 'Follow me! And most importantly, breathe.'

Like you'd forget to breathe, thinks Leila. But when Liv starts to lift her arms and lower them, bending at her waist and twisting side to side, Leila concentrates so hard on following she does, in fact, forget to breathe.

The first time they bend, Leila can only just reach her toes with her fingertips, but by the third cycle her hands are flat against the grippy paint of the deck. They walk their hands from side to side, and Leila feels a stretch in her sides and back. Places she didn't know were knotted begin to unknot.

At the end, Liv brings her hands together at her heart, like she's praying. Liv closes her eyes, and tells them to breathe in and out deeply, into their bellies, not their shoulders. This makes no sense to Leila until she tries it: drawing the cold sea air deeper than normal, feeling her back seeming to become cavernous. She closes her eyes, too.

It is a very different kind of dark from nighttime or sleep. The reds of her eyelids glow, and as her breaths go on and on, they become colours, blues and greys, like the fox, and she tracks them around her body, entering her mouth and feeding not only her lungs but also her arms, her legs, her fingers and toes. She feels warm from the core of her, cool from the air. She feels out of her body, and inside it.

'Namaste,' says Liv, breaking Leila's trance. Mum and Matty repeat the word back to her. Leila attempts it too.

'Namustard.'

Liv lets out a hoot of laughter. 'That's a good one!'

Leila blushes. Mum says, 'Namaste. It means, the light in me recognises the light in you.'

Leila's neck feels longer. She hadn't noticed how her shoulders had lived by her ears for the last few days. Who knew breathing could do all that?

'Shall we see where Miso is?' Mum asks.

'Sure,' Matty turns to Leila. 'Want to come see our set-up?'

She follows them back down the staircase, to a room about triple the size of where they are sleeping. A table is fixed to the floor with large hexagonal bolts, and benches line the walls. The map with Miso's movements to date is taped on the largest wall.

Matty pulls an ancient-looking laptop out of a drawer under the bench and opens the lid.

'Takes a while to power up,' he explains, pressing a button that makes the laptop purr like a cat. 'But this gives us the most accurate reading. It all runs off GPS, so wherever we are we can track her.'

'The collar is a little bigger than I'd like,' says Mum. 'But it's light, and she seems to have had no trouble with it.'

'Why are you tracking her?' says Leila, and Mum and Matty look at each other and laugh.

'That's a good question,' says Mum. 'For the longest time I didn't have a good enough answer. Curiosity isn't enough to get grants any more. Everything is outcome-based. But when Miso started walking, we knew our tracking had paid off.'

'Literally,' says Matty.

'Everything I've worked on, even back home in Damascus, has been about climate,' continues Mum. 'The air we breathe, the water that flows around the world, the seasons and how they change. And we are living through some of the most rapid change this planet has ever experienced. It's changing everything: what flowers grow, where people live and what they wage wars about. That Miso is using the sea ice is a perfect little snapshot of this. That ice is vanishing. Migration is becoming harder—' Mum breaks off, shakes her head.

Leila has never heard Mum talk like this. Not about home or her work. Hearing the name of their home city leave her mouth was like an electric shock against Leila's skin.

'My point is,' says Mum. 'Miso offers so many questions in miniature. Maybe even some answers. She's a scavenger, she has to take all she can get, go where she needs to, to find food or territory or a mate. Safety. She's not so different from a person, really.'

If Matty weren't there, Leila wonders if she would have been brave enough to ask, then. The question that's always been there, but growing stronger and sharper in the past few days. *Why did you leave me?*

But then the laptop bings loudly, and Matty cheers. 'Here we go!'

He turns the screen so Leila can see. There are only two icons on the grainy screen: one called GPS, the other a familiar blue bird. Mum groans.

'Twitter? Really?'

90

'It's a condition of the funding,' says Matty. 'Outreach, engagement, accessibility.'

He double clicks the icon and navigates to the homepage. Under the handle @MisoTheFox is a photo of the fox, the one Liv showed her back in the small apartment. The header is a badly lit photo of Mum and Liv, their arms around each other, snow goggles obscuring their eyes. It's still obvious it's them because of Mum's lipstick and Liv's wild curls escaping. They are surrounded by a dazzlement of ice and snow.

'Look,' says Matty, 'I've been backdating Miso's journey, adding to this online map people can follow.'

He scrolls down to show them a handful of tweets. Leila glances at the follower count. Three.

'You're not following anyone?' Leila says. 'You need to follow some people, so they'll maybe follow you back. It makes you look like a spam account otherwise.'

'Why do you know about social media?' asks Mum.

'Mona,' says Leila. 'But she's more into Instagram and TikTok.'

'What's TikTok?'

'You're too old to care,' says Leila and Mum mimes mock-offence. 'Can I?'

Matty moves aside so Leila can sit down in front of the keyboard. The keys are arranged differently from Mona's MacBook, and there's an actual separate mouse instead of a trackpad, but after a few false starts Leila manages to start searching on the Explore tab.

Leila follows Mum's work Twitter handle. She searches for names with Arctic in, and Fox, and follows National Geographic. By the time she's done, they're following about thirty relevant people. As they watch, their follower account clicks over into four.

'You should tweet some of them,' says Leila. 'And use hashtags, if engagement is important.'

'Sure,' says Matty. 'Thanks, Leila. Any ideas for hashtags?'

'Just things people follow, like "wildlife" and "foxes". And maybe "Where's Miso"?' says Leila, 'when you tweet where she is with the link to the map.'

'Great,' says Matty. 'You're our social media manager now!'

'OK,' says Leila, shrugging uncomfortably.

'Thanks Leila,' says Mum, resting her arm across her shoulders. 'Now, shall we see where Miso actually is?'

'Whale!'

The shout comes about noon, the sun high overhead.

'Whale!'

Liv throws herself against the railing, bending almost in half. She points, and Leila dislodges herself from where she's sat by the stern with her hands tucked under her armpits for warmth, and hurries to where Liv stands whooping. For a moment all Leila can see is blue-grey water and ice-white foam. But then suddenly, impossibly, something begins to rise from the depths.

A long snout, angular fins, its back crisscrossed with black lines.

'Minke!' says Liv. 'An old one, judging by those battle scars. See the white band?'

Leila can barely take in what she says. A whale. A real-life whale. Leila widens her eyes, trying to drink it in as snorts of water issue from the hole in its head. It is close enough to see the texture of its skin, pitted with scars, almost geological.

'One, two, three!' says Liv triumphantly. 'She's exhibiting textbook behaviour. Isn't she beautiful?'

The whale skims the surface and then dives again. It's about half the length of the boat, the water playing with its size and colours. It swims just below the surface again, then comes up. Leila wishes she could touch it. It arches its back, and its tail flips up.

'She's going to dive!' exclaims Liv, and sure enough, this time when the whale darns beneath the surface, Leila sees it vanish down, down, down, and finally she can't see it at all.

It was the work of a moment, but Leila's heart is racing. Her skin feels electrified. She has never been so close to something so wild, and finally she thinks she feels, just a little bit, of what makes Mum want to follow Miso across the sea ice. When the whale had dived, Leila wanted to too, just to spend a moment longer with her.

She's reached the land of bears. She smells them in every step – fighting males, learning cubs. She traces the scent of one across a week, tracks him to a break in the ice.

He is diving, and she waits, watches, digging herself deeper
into the snow. He erupts from the water with a seal, and there is
a struggle. There is blood. There is a meal she needs.

But she has to wait.

The bear drags the seal clear of the exposed edge of ice. She
follows, licking what she can from the ground, and he takes her
to a beach.

The bear keeps all other prey away. It eats the seal to its bones,
and moves on. Fox waits until he is truly gone, and approaches,
inch by inch, towards the food. Her snout finds the last morsels,
life saving and fresh. She strips the meat from the bone, the bone
from the marrow, chews until her belly is full.

She keeps to the beach. She waits. She watches. She tries not
to be hunted, as she looks for something to hunt.

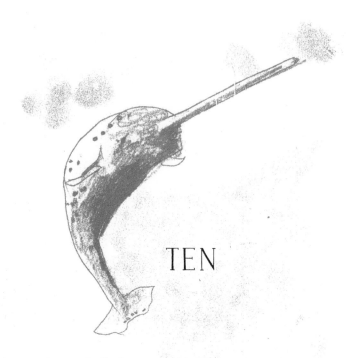

TEN

It's amazing to Leila how quickly you can get used to something. Within three days, she falls asleep easily in their bunk room, memories of the detention centre tucked deeper away again, the knocking memories raised by the rocking of the boat suppressed, her body adjusting to the confines of the bunk, the gentle rise and fall of Liv's snores.

She stops feeling sick, and looks forward to Liv's yoga sessions. The breath moving grey-blue through her body, more and more in her mind's eye like the fox they track, moving the red marker and thread millimetre by millimetre across the map. She's becoming invested in the animal as the days pass, speaking with Matty about how Miso's fur is thick and multi-layered, shedding with the seasons from fluffy to short, how they suspect she is walking to find a mate, and when she does, how they will mate for life. Miso is taking on a personality for Leila. To her, Miso is brave like Amma, neat like Mona. Maybe even seeking something, like her.

Leila even gets used to seeing Mum, to talking to her, to hugging her and sharing jokes. The one thing she can't adjust to are the memories that keep coming: Mum holding her under the armpits to pick fresh figs from overhanging branches; Basbousa purring loudly next to her ear, his whiskers tickling her cheek. They come like a torrent sometimes, like a wall of water rushing at her, pulling her under. With them arrive feelings so big she can't fit them all inside her head: sadness and happiness and the feeling Britt described, of a lost life, a half life it is easier to forget.

Britt herself is a rare appearance, coming on deck only at mealtimes. Leila thought maybe they would get closer, but ever since Leila agreed to do Liv's yoga session, it feels like she's crossed over a divide, and Britt has closed the gate after her.

'We saw a whale,' Leila had told her that first day, coming down to find her in the bunkroom, reading a book.

'Wow,' said Britt flatly.

'A female minke.'

'Double wow.'

'Are you OK?'

Britt didn't look up from her book. 'I'm fine.'

'OK.' If they'd known each other better, Leila maybe would have pushed more. But instead she had backed out, closed the door as quietly as she could, and retreated back on deck.

Each day after breakfast Leila helps Matty with the Twitter account, and soon they have ten followers, then twenty, a milestone that causes Mum and Liv as much excitement as when Mona got ten thousand on TikTok for her make-up hacks.

'It would be better if we had more photos,' says Leila. 'People love photos of animals.'

'We only have these,' says Matty, tapping the same images they've used again and again. 'But soon we will be within eyesight of her, and we can take lots.'

By now, Miso's walked one thousand two hundred miles from her beach in Svalbard, sometimes spending a couple of days in one place, sometimes walking for nearly a full day and a night without pause. One day she walks sixty-two miles, another she covers eighty-five.

The map on the wall starts to take on new meaning for Leila. Usually when she lives with something for a while, like the poster on her wall of a cactus with a speech bubble saying, 'I'll never desert you', it becomes part of the wallpaper. But the map seems to get more interesting with attention, not less.

She notices the faint lines showing where the ice used to freeze to, retreating every year. She sees the border lines jostling for space across the Arctic: Russia and America and Norway and Denmark and Canada and Greenland, their territories circling each other like wolves. And the thin thread of the fox crossing all the borders, walking on water.

And how far Miso is walking: that becomes incredible, too. Now Leila can track the boat's progress, inch by inch over the blue Norwegian Sea, she can better understand what a mile means. And the fox, Mum tells her, is small as a house cat.

'Small as Basbousa,' she says, a sad glint in her eyes. 'Imagine that, four small paws walking all that way.'

'She must be lonely,' says Leila.

Liv sighs and throws an arm around her shoulders, shaking her gently. 'Too sentimental. Miso doesn't think of herself as lonely, only alone. She doesn't think of herself as small, only as more or less powerful than the animals around her. She doesn't feel the same way humans do, doesn't see the world the same.'

'I know!' says Leila defensively.

'I wonder if you do,' says Liv, and there's something more serious in her usually jovial face. 'You must never fall in love with a wild animal. At best, they will never love you back, and at worst they will break your heart when they die.'

Mum mimics spitting, to ward off the evil eye again, but Leila stops herself doing the same.

'I speak from experience,' says Liv. 'My first placement, I

tracked a polar bear family. Three cubs. One died, one was killed by its father—'

'Shhh!' says Mum, covering Leila's ears. 'Leila doesn't need to hear this.'

'She does! I tell you, you're too soft, you meteorologists. These are the facts of the wild. It is all about survival.'

'And Miso is a survivor,' says Mum, bringing her hand down on the table making Leila jump.

Before anyone can say anything else, Mum has turned on her heel and walked out. Leila follows, up the metal steps to the deck.

She finds Mum at the bow, her bob whipping in the wind. Neither of them has remembered their coats, and Leila's teeth start to chatter instantly. She comes to stand right beside Mum, who takes a moment to notice her. Her face is shiny with tears.

Leila feels her tummy tighten. It is always hard to know how to comfort someone who is crying, especially if you don't know them very well. Extra especially when they are your mum.

'D-don't look,' says Mum through clattering teeth.

'I've s-seen you cry bef-fore,' says Leila, stamping her feet. 'When we left Basb-b-bousa.'

Mum frowns. 'You remember that?'

Leila snuggles closer into Mum's side, and Mum wraps her against her waist. Together their warmth offers some barrier to the cold. 'Yes.'

'You remember home?'

'Some of it.'

'You remember leaving home?'

'More of it, lately.'

Mum takes in a shuddering breath. 'Oh, Leila. I was worried . . . about the boat . . . I did wonder. But I hoped you were too little to carry all that with you. Would you . . .' the catch in her voice now has nothing to do with the cold. 'Would you like to talk about it?'

Leila feels like the boat is unfolding under her feet, expanding like an accordion. Here it is, an invitation to open that painful flood of memories further, to ask her questions. But what if she doesn't like the answers?

Mum's body is tense, like she's bracing for a blow. So Leila shakes her head.

'Not right now.'

Mum's muscles relax, and she kisses the top of Leila's head. 'But when you want to, we will – all right, La-La?'

It is only later, her numb fingers warming back into feeling around a cup of powdery hot chocolate, that Leila realises Mum had used her pet name, and Leila hadn't minded.

That evening, after dinner, they finally call Amma and Mona on the boat's satellite phone. Even on speaker, the connection is a bit crackly and far away, but this is a blessing when a bored-sounding Mona picks up the house phone and shrieks at the top of her lungs when she hears Leila say, 'Hi, Mon.'

Amma comes on the line, and Leila imagines them both crowding around the phone. Her tummy twists a little with missing.

'How are you? Are you eating enough? How is Tromsø?'

Leila glances uncertainly at Mum, who answers, 'It's great, great.'

Leila frowns. Is she not telling them where they are?

'How are you finding it, Leila?'

'Fine,' she says, and because Mum seems to be trying to telepathically bore into her head to say, *don't tell them where we are*, adds only, 'cold.'

'Are you wearing your vest?'

'Of course.'

'We've been calling your mobile, but it's never going through,' says Mona accusingly. 'Are you blocking me?'

'Never!' says Leila, not wanting to explain about the banana. 'It just doesn't work here.'

'I knew it,' grumbles Mona. 'That guy at the phone shop seemed dodgy to me. We should have got a different sim.'

'It's fine,' says Leila. 'We can call you from . . . from here.'

'Give me the number, habibti,' says Amma. 'I want to be able to call more.'

Leila looks at Mum. The lies feel sticky and sour on her tongue. Mum leans over the phone.

'It's easier if we call,' says Mum. 'We're out a lot.'

'All right,' says Amma, blindly trusting. Leila can imagine Mona raising her eyebrow sceptically, but she doesn't say anything.

'How are you all?' says Mum.

'Fine, we are fine. Missing our Leila. We are looking forward to having her back with us.'

'She's having a good time. Aren't you, Leila?' says Mum.

'Yeah, I am, Amma.'

'Good,' says Amma. 'You take care of her for us.'

'Of course,' snaps Mum. 'She's my daughter, Zaha.'

Mona starts to say something, her voice high with temper, but Amma talks over her, her voice soothing. 'Yes, yes, we know.'

'We have to go,' says Mum briskly, and before Leila can say a proper goodbye she disconnects the call.

'I'd forgotten how nosy they are,' she says, a little spitefully. Leila has to look down to hide her face, because the same rage she'd felt while trampling the Arctic Institute gardens is bubbling inside her. 'Do you want to do a last Miso update before bed?'

It's all Leila can do to shake her head no, before she stumbles out of the room and into the dark safety of their bunk room.

ELEVEN

'Hey,' says Britt.

Leila doesn't trust her voice not to shake. Britt sets aside her book, and rolls on to her side to look at Leila.

'What's up?'

'Why would I tell you?' snaps Leila. Britt holds her hands up in mock surrender. 'Sorry. Just my mum.'

'Ah,' says Britt. 'If you want, we can talk about it? Not now, but when they are asleep.'

'We'll wake them up.'

'Not here,' says Britt. 'Just stay awake, I'll show you. Is your coat in the locker? Good. Keep your jumper on, and your socks. They normally fall asleep in an hour or so. You just have to make sure you don't.'

*

Almost exactly an hour after Mum and Liv climbed into bed, Leila feels Britt nudge her with her foot. Holding her breath, she swings herself over the edge of the bunk, socked feet feeling for the ladder rungs, and follows Britt out of the door. The older girl puts a sock over the latch to smother the sound of it closing, and opens the lockers so they can fetch their coats and boots. They creep up the steps, and out on to the deck.

It will never not be strange, Leila decides, that what greets them was not pitch black, but a sort of dusk light dotted with stars, faded as old pennies. Overhead birds swoop and cry.

'This is as dark as it gets,' says Britt, leading her to the back of the boat, behind the wheelhouse. One of the crew members, Lenny, is at the wheel, and he gives them a cheery wave, showing no surprise to see them out of bed.

'Brought your friend?' he asks.

'Thought it was about time,' says Britt.

She drags two large ice boxes to the very edge of the boat, against the railing, and they sit watching the sky a moment.

'So, you do this every night?' says Leila. 'Is that why you're always sleeping in the day?'

'That, and I'm avoiding Mamma.' Britt burrows her chin into her coat. 'I thought you could do with a place and time to avoid yours, too.'

Leila struggles with herself. Yes, she does. She wants to tell

Britt about the phone call, and how angry it made her, and how sometimes she thought that maybe Mum wasn't a very nice person. But Britt had withdrawn from her so sharply, it felt strange to suddenly trust her with her deepest thoughts.

'Listen,' says Britt, as though reading her mind. 'I know I've not been the nicest. I find it hard sometimes . . . I get angry. It's not anything you've done. It's all about Mamma. This interest she has in everything around her, but me. You know she's not asked me one question about school since that first day? Nothing about my friends or what I like to read or what music I listen to. She knows the names of every whale but nothing about me.'

Leila feels a similar shiver as she had that first night, when they'd talked on the sofas. Like Britt was reaching out and pulling all Leila's own fears and feelings out, and fitting them into words.

'My mum's the same,' she says at last, letting the traitorous thought out. 'It's all about Miso and her research. And then today, finally, I thought maybe she was ready to talk about it all. Why she left me to come here. But even though she said we could talk, I knew she didn't actually want to. We called my aunt and cousin in London, and she made me lie about being here, on the boat.'

Britt scrunches up her nose. 'That's weird.'

'Right? And then when they sounded worried, because I think they could tell something wasn't right, she just hung up.'

'That's not fair,' says Britt.

'I wasn't ready to say goodbye,' says Leila, her indignation rising again. 'She didn't even give me time to ask how they were, how Mona's summer job's going, how Amma's back is. I wanted to tell them about the Twitter page, but of course Mum wouldn't have liked that, because she's not even telling them where we are!'

Little sparks are popping in front of Leila's eyes. Britt is rubbing her arm, murmuring comforting words, but she can't hear them through the roar in her ears.

Almost panting, Leila takes a deep, steadying breath, like Liv taught her. Slowly, the sparks recede, and the tightness in her chest loosens.

'Sorry,' says Leila, embarrassed.

'Don't be,' says Britt. 'That's a lot. I thought you were having a good time, hanging out with Mamma and your mum. Seemed like you liked it, and I guess I felt left out.'

'Maybe you could help me with the Twitter feed? Miso's sweet, and it is kind of amazing how far she's walked.'

'Sure,' says Britt. 'I'd like that.'

'And the yoga's quite good actually.'

Britt wrinkles her nose. 'Don't push it.'

Leila laughs. 'OK. But maybe we can do this again?'

Britt smirks. 'You don't even know what *this* is yet. I'll show you.'

Britt swings her leg over the railing, and Leila's heart thuds hard until she notices that beneath them is not simply sea, but a ladder, leading to the smaller vessel she'd noticed on the first day. Britt drops down into it, and it sinks lower in the water. She waves Leila down impatiently. 'Come on!'

The drop is about six feet, but right now it looks much higher. Britt is staring at her, so Leila slips another Werther's Original from its wrapping, sticks it between her gritted teeth and swings out on to the ladder, the metal rungs icy even through her gloves. She keeps her eyes fixed straight ahead, on the barnacled hull of the boat, taking the rungs one at a time and sucking on the sweet.

Finally, she feels Britt's hands close over her ankle and guide her into the bottom of the boat. Leila is so glad to be off the ladder she plonks herself down on the seat feeling triumphant. Being down so low gives an entirely new perspective, making the sea feel more immediate, more real and expansive. The sky is starting to darken to a pitch Leila hasn't seen in days.

Britt bends under the seat and pulls out a fishing rod. A lure dances over the hook, silver and glinting.

'Don't you need bait?'

'No. It would freeze. You need them wriggling. Better to use the lure here.'

Britt casts off expertly, sending the line flicking into the lulling waves. 'And now we wait.'

'How come you fish? Is it a Norwegian thing?'

Britt laughs. Her face is more relaxed than Leila's ever seen it. 'My dad taught me. We fish in the fjord near our cabin.'

'In the Lofoten Islands?' says Leila, carefully.

'Exactly! Your pronunciation has got much better.'

'*Takk.*'

'*Værsågod.*'

'Bless you.'

Britt snorts. 'Now shhh. I have to listen to the line,' says Britt. 'Here, feel.'

She hands Leila the rod. There is more pressure on it than she was expecting, with the drag of the boat and the currents.

'Put your finger here.' Britt places Leila's index finger on the line. 'Feel it humming? And when it gets higher or lower, there's a change, which means a fish.'

It's become easier to be silent. At home she's always listening to music, watching YouTube, borrowing Amma's iPad to play games. She likes noise, found it uncomfortable to be alone with her thoughts at night or with nothing to watch during the day. But with Liv's breathing and the sea, it feels like she's coming back to her body in a way that used to feel easy as a young kid.

Lulled by the waves, she lets her eyes go unfocused. Lately the memories have felt less like assaults and more like she can invite them in, and now she sinks into a sticky Damascus night, fireworks crackling through the sky, their roof terrace full of neighbours and friends, all of them dancing and laughing. A girl who was her best friend but now whose name she can't remember. Their neighbour who now cares for Basbousa swinging Mum around in a wild spin. So much light and colour Leila felt full of it, like a firework herself, sparking with happiness.

Something breaks the surface of the water, snapping Leila's gaze back into focus. It's like a rock has sprouted suddenly from the sea. Suddenly Leila gets a sensation of vertigo, worse than when she'd descended the ladder. She understands, from her head to her stomach, that below them is not only water, but whales and fish and sharks, unseen but there. She grasps for Britt's arm.

'What was that?'

'Could be anything,' shrugs Britt. 'Orca, minke, walrus.'

Suddenly there's a tug on the rod. Leila feels it jolt through her arms, and almost loses her grip. She tightens, wrestling with it, as Britt whoops.

'Turn the reel!'

Leila does so, feeling the weight through her arms. Her muscles strain. The rod bends.

'Seems a good size,' says Britt. 'Cod, hopefully! You're doing great!'

But then the shape appears again, and this time Britt sees it too. 'Uh-oh,' she says. 'A thief! Reel faster!'

Leila redoubles her efforts on the rod, but the line goes slack, and Leila is propelled backwards, thumping hard off the seat. Her heart is racing.

Britt helps her up and they both scan the sea. There is nothing, and nothing, and then a round, dappled head rises from the waves. Coal-black eyes shine at them, and clasped in a wide mouth, a fish flops helplessly.

'Leopard seal,' says Britt. 'Cheeky beasts.'

The seal flips suddenly below the waves, sending a spray of water into the boat. The cold shock of it makes them gasp, and Britt shouts a laugh. 'Next time! Seal one, us nil!'

Leila's heart is still racing, but she laughs too. Her blood feels very hot, pouring around her body. She feels the same sensation she remembers from the rooftop. Joy.

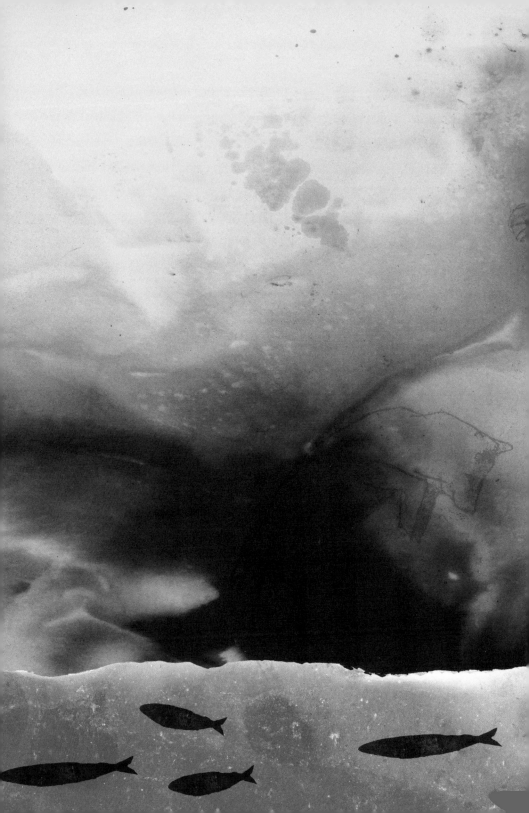

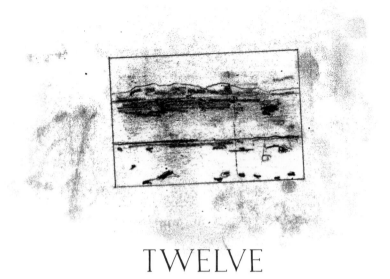

TWELVE

In school history lessons, when Ms Matthews had talked about sea voyages lasting months, Leila had only half listened, and not at all understood what that sort of time at sea meant. But now, seeing a thin white line on the horizon, she feels some sort of recognition of how it must have been to sight land after all that time on the water. Even though it has taken less than a week to reach Greenland, Leila feels a swelling excitement.

It is a perfect blue day, crisp as a cooking apple and just as sharp. Matty takes a photo for Twitter, of the sky and the horizon and the sea in perfect thirds. Captain Johansson agrees that they can take the landing craft out on the calm water, so Leila goes with Matty to check Miso's exact location.

'Miso is there, at this beach,' he says, pointing at the spot on the map, which is now mere miles from the boat. 'Don't get your hopes up too high but she's been there barely a day, and moving at a real pace before that, so we may catch her while she rests.'

Butterflies fill Leila's stomach.

She sends a tweet to their ninety-two followers.

First landing on the Arctic today. Soon we will be able to see Miso with our own eyes. She's already walked 1,800 miles – link in bio for the map. Fingers crossed for photos! #WhereIsMiso #ArcticFox #ArcticVoyage #LandAhoy

She attaches the photo of the horizon that Matty took. As soon as she posts it, they get a like.

Mum, Liv and Britt are already in the landing craft, laps piled high with binoculars and thermoses and rucksacks, even though Captain Johansson is explaining gruffly that they can't expect to stay on land long, not with a weather front coming.

'I know all about weather fronts,' snaps Mum, with the first flash of temper she's ever shown the captain. 'We're clear for eight hours at least.'

'It'll take an hour to land,' warns the captain, shrugging. 'But if you are sure.'

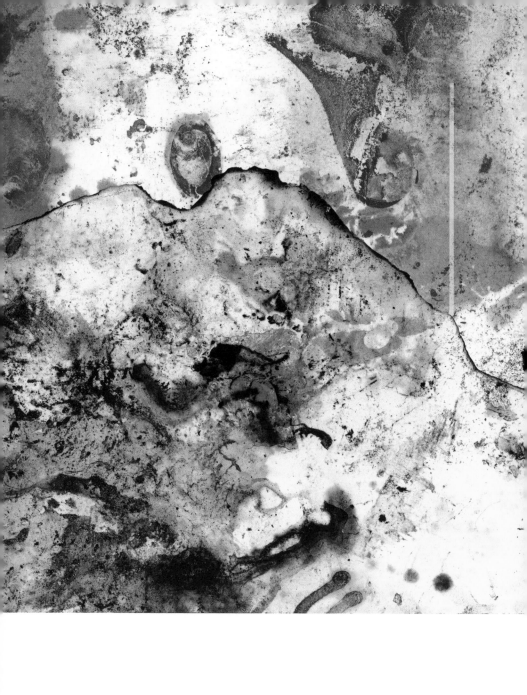

'We are,' says Liv, and, spotting Leila, waves her impatiently
on board. 'Come on, let's get going!'

The boat feels tiny and cramped with them and Lenny on board, lower and more unstable in the water. Lenny casts off the rope and starts the engine, and soon they are moving, faster than Leila was expecting, across the sea towards the white stripe of land.

'First time setting foot this far north!' shouts Mum, over the roar of the wind and the motor. 'How exciting!'

Leila hasn't forgiven her for the phone call, and rolls her eyes at Britt, who has looped her arm through hers for warmth. Britt rolls her own back, but she's grinning wide, and Leila can tell she's excited and trying not to show it.

As they get close enough to the land to make out details, it's like something from a David Attenborough documentary – sheer sidings of ice sliced through by crevasses, mini waterfalls sluicing from them, and black rock gleaming through like glimpses into the underworld.

Lenny steers them to a shelving jut of land, helps them from the boat. Leila examines the ground. The Arctic. It's muckier up close, the pure white of the ice mixed with grains of black rock and thick and sturdy-looking tufts of grass.

The air is sharp, tiny needles of cold stitching up her throat. The ground is hard-going, gritty and slippery. But once they reach the top of the slope, Britt, Liv and Mum barely panting and Leila entirely out of breath, she forgets the tightness in her chest.

Below them is spread a vast tundra of white. From their vantage point they can see the crevices lacing along the ice into the distance, a patchwork of gaps through which channels of sea run and lap and sway. Some of the pieces of ice seem barely tethered, bobbing in the water like floating islands. It goes, on and on, into the distance. All the way to the top of the world – which Leila is learning is all a matter of perspective anyway.

They walk for perhaps a half hour, and Leila is glad of her snow goggles, filtering the brightness into more manageable shades of grey and blue, showing the cracks in the ice more clearly. When they reach the beach, Mum and Liv duck almost comically behind a large rock, binoculars at the ready.

Liv yanks Britt down beside her, and Leila crouches next to Mum. 'Any sign?'

'Shhh!' hisses Mum, but Liv leans around her and shakes her head. 'Must have moved on.'

'Al'ama!' says Mum. Leila flinches. She's never heard her swear in Arabic before. It feels even worse, her anger more pure. 'This is why we needed the portable tracker!'

'There was no money for it,' soothes Liv.

'There's something there,' says Britt, squinting through the binoculars and pointing. 'By the shore. I think it's maybe . . . bones.'

Mum freezes, and Liv inhales sharply. 'Where?'

Britt points again, and Mum leaps to her feet, striding towards the spot.

'Amani!' shouts Liv. 'If it's a fresh kill, there could be a bear!'

Panic fills Leila. A bear? Mum looks very small and exposed out there on the beach in her bright blue coat. She pushes herself up and after Mum, ignoring Liv's repeated shout.

The pebbles slip about beneath her feet, and she stumbles a few times, just keeping her balance; the boat has been good practice for being on unstable ground. She catches Mum up just before she reaches the place Britt pointed. Mum lets out a sound that could be a sob or a laugh, and it is only when she turns around, beaming, that Leila can be sure which.

'Picked clean,' she calls to Liv. 'Come see!'

Leila reaches Mum's side, and she's glad it's so cold, because there's no smell, no rot. A collection of very white bones is strewn across the pebbles. Here and there greyish fur clings to the skeleton, but it is for the most part as Mum said: clean.

Liv arrives huffing. 'You must be more careful!' she snaps. Leila has never heard her angry before. 'Polar bears are no joke, and we left the gun in the boat.'

'You wouldn't shoot one, would you?' says Leila, shocked.

'Better it than you,' Liv says severely. She bends low over the bones. 'Bearded seal, I reckon. See the fusing?'

'So a polar bear killed it?' says Leila.

'A few days ago. And judging by the disarrangement, probably elsewhere. Miso likely trailed the bear, and when it had eaten its fill, she dragged it here to feed.' Liv squints at the remains. 'I

126

think you can see the difference in the bite marks. There are the bear's teeth, and there are Miso's.'

Looking so closely at these bones gives Leila a funny feeling, the way chicken bones don't. Why is that, she wonders? She can see what Liv means. There are deep indentations, showing a mouth wide as Leila's arm is long. Then smaller, daintier nibbles.

'I hope we didn't scare her off,' frowns Liv, looking around. 'She needs all the food she can get, the rate she's going.'

Mum is already striding further along the beach, camera clutched hopefully in her hands.

'The racket she's making,' sighs Liv. She smiles ruefully at Leila. 'I love your mother, but she doesn't quite realise her impact sometimes.'

Leila wonders dimly whether to defend Mum, but the truth of Liv's words is undeniable. She watches Mum's retreating back, the confidence of her stride, the easiness with which she forges on alone, leaving them behind.

The bones have made Leila sad. She suddenly feels very small in the world, and like every living thing is just scraping to survive and she has gone all her life not really thinking about it. Mona, though, she thinks about it. Leila has heard her nightmares. She knows the crossing to England was difficult, dangerous. The detention centre was horrid, but it was dry and warm. She is grateful her memories won't let her go there. Not every box has to be opened.

She remembers their smell.

The beach is not safe any more.

It is no easy thing for a fox, to abandon a territory.

The sky is full of crackling, tugging at her fur. The snow comes, the wind howls. Fox finds a hollow, makes herself small. The cold is around her like a cage.

She hides her nose in her tail.

Waits for it to pass.

THIRTEEN

The storm blows over fast, according to Captain Johansson, but it doesn't feel fast at all to Leila. Being below deck on a rolling boat was not ideal, and for the first time Leila came face to face with the toilet bowl.

'That's it,' said Liv encouragingly. 'Get it all out! Make sure you flush each time there's a pause, though.'

She was standing right outside, offering helpful advice and Leila wished she would go away until the boat tilted to what felt like entirely sideways. Leila let out a muted scream.

'Don't worry about that! It's what these boats are designed for,' said Liv, 'it'll bob upright like a cork. But see why I told you to flush?'

Leila mumbled a heartfelt thanks.

The storm knocks out their communications, their satellite tracking and internet. Leila feels sick that she has no idea where Miso is. Mum seems to share the feeling, and not for the first time Leila's jealousy rises, that her mum seems to care more about hourly checking on a fox than even weekly checking in on Leila. She wonders if Mona and Amma will be worrying they haven't heard from her.

They are mostly confined to their cabin, and the atmosphere is sour. Britt's animosity towards Liv is almost overwhelming, as though her mother had conjured the storm herself.

Leila wishes Britt would go a bit easier on her, especially as Leila actually finds her breath exercises very useful once her stomach is empty. That feeling she'd had standing on the snow looking at the bones, of the wideness of the world and her smallness in it, hasn't left entirely, but it fades the most when she focuses on being all breath and nothing else. Just breath, moving in, pushing out.

Finally, Captain Johansson knocks on their door. It rouses Leila from a restless half sleep, her tongue sticking to the roof of her mouth. She doesn't immediately know where she is, and sits up, banging her head on the ceiling.

'It has passed,' he says. 'Would you like to take some breakfast?'

Going on deck after being in their cabin so long is like coming outside in the middle of the day after being at the cinema. The sky is a dazzlement of purest white, and Leila wishes she'd brought her snow goggles. The air is so cold it makes her gasp. It is a moment before she realises what feels so wrong about standing there: not the light or the cold, but the stillness of the boat. The swaying comes mostly from her own weakened legs and empty tummy.

Mum swears in Arabic. 'We are locked?'

Leila follows her gaze, and sees what she means. The sea is gone. In its place, a shimmering, endless sheet of ice, indistinguishable from the sky at the horizon, all of it smudged together by an icy thumb.

'It is always a risk,' shrugs Captain Johansson. 'It is the Arctic.'

'But at this time of year?' says Liv. 'The Gulf Stream surely pushes it clear.'

'Ten years ago, yes. Even five. But it is less and less easy to predict now. Everything is changing. This is why your fox is using the ice, yes?'

'Can't we break it? I thought this boat was equipped for this sort of situation.' Mum's voice is barely contained, rising in peaks sharp as the frozen waves below.

Captain Johansson smiles wryly. 'We are. We have supplies. We must wait a few days.'

'No,' Mum is shaking her head. 'We are so close to her. We can ski.'

'Of course you can,' says the captain, frowning now. 'But the effort is so much greater, and the risk.'

'Our funding is to study her,' says Mum. 'Locating her is only part of it. We must observe her. What she is eating, her interactions with other animals.'

'You know we are in Danish and international waters here,' says the captain. 'But soon we will reach Canadian seas, and I thought—'

'You thought wrong,' snaps Mum. 'I can't study her from a boat. I'm going on the ice.'

'I would not advise it, but I cannot stop you.' Captain Johansson looks from Mum to Liv, as if appealing for help.

'Good,' says Mum. 'We'll leave in an hour.'

Mum picks up a pastry, striding to the back of the boat with it, her jaw set. Liv follows her. Britt and Leila look at each other nervously.

'Matty,' says Britt quietly, once Captain Johansson has taken his own pastry and slunk off to the wheelhouse. 'Are you sure this is a good idea?'

'No,' says Matty in a low voice. 'But I have to back my boss.'

Leila watches them load backpacks and measure themselves against ski poles. Britt insisted she go with them, and only Leila will be left behind. They have climbed down the ladder on the outside of the boat, on to the sea ice and, as Leila watches them getting ready to go, hot tears scald her eyes, blurring them to wraiths. She's wearing her goggles now, so no one can see, but surely Mum must realise how she's feeling? She knows it's not Mum's fault that she can't ski but, yet again, it is so easy for her mum to leave her behind.

'Will you be OK on the boat?' says Mum without even looking at Leila, and in a tone that suggests she doesn't really care.

'Yeah sure, I'll stay,' Leila steadies her voice. 'That's clearly what you wanted anyway.'

'Leila—'

She flinches away from Mum's outstretched hand.

'Go!' she shouts, her throat raw with cold. 'You're good at that.'

But then Mum's gloved hand closes on her shoulder and all her rage leaves her. She feels only immensely, crushingly sad.

Mum turns her to face her, lifting her goggles and Leila's. The ice is blindingly white, but Mum's face shows clear against it, skin the smoothest golden-brown. Mum wipes her cheeks with her scratchy gloves, and pulls Leila tight against her. Leila can hear her heart, beating just as hard as her own.

'We can both stay,' murmurs Mum into her hat. 'OK? We'll both stay.'

Leila relaxes into the hug. She feels, for the first time in forever, the full weight of Mum's love. She knows she would stay, give up following Miso, for Leila.

'There's no need,' says a gentle voice. Leila looks up to see Matty, gesturing behind them. Still in their hug, Leila and Mum shuffle to see where he's pointing. The sledge is empty.

'We can carry the equipment,' says Matty. Leila sees he is loaded like a packhorse with various bags, the gun pushed to one side. 'It won't be comfy, but with all four of us pulling it will be easy enough. We need our social media manager! That's if you want to come?'

Leila feels an enormous rush of warmth towards the man. 'Yeah. I want to come. If it's OK?'

'Of course it is,' beams Mum, and she lets go of Leila. Her relief is obvious, and amongst Leila's excitement and gratitude, still sits the sharp spike of hurt.

'It'll be good,' says Matty. 'You can navigate.'

Leila takes the map and compass from him. A week ago, she wouldn't have been confident about holding the map up the right way, let alone reading a compass, but now the lines and numbers and colours make sense to her, the compass's spinning needle a language she understands. She climbs on to the sledge's bed, made of stretched fabric, and Matty ties her in. The four others arrange themselves in front of the sled, and he links them together with ropes.

We are like your huskies, yes?' he laughs, and howls at the white sky. Britt and Liv join in, and as they set off at walking pace across the frozen sea, Leila feels her cheeks might crack from smiling so wide.

FOURTEEN

They progress fast enough across the sea ice, but the sledge is not designed to carry people, and unlike the equipment Leila is not nestled in layers of shock absorbent foam. She feels every jolt of the sledge ricochet through her bones, each vertebra of her spine rattling, teeth chattering in her skull as they ski over the locked waves.

'All right?' calls Matty over his shoulder. He is attached closest to her, with Liv in front of him, then Britt, then Mum at the front. She's glad he's nearest to her – he doesn't get impatient when she checks and rechecks the compass, the map. 'We will reach the more established sea ice soon. It will be smoother.'

They move like one, legs and arms working in unison, Leila

their eyes and nose, scenting the way. Seeing Mum ski is like watching a fish walk on land – completely unexpected and entirely strange. But Mum is good at it, that much is clear, setting a determined pace.

Finally, the ground changes. The ice is whiter somehow, which Leila guesses means it's thicker. As Matty promised, it's definitely smoother, and Leila looks up, watching the white sky pass over. Even the clouds here are different from anything she's seen in London, like perpetual fog made into strings, laid over a brilliant blue-white sky.

She thinks of Mona and Amma in their neat-as-a-pin house with doilies on all the tables, coasters used diligently on every surface, and the smell of garlic always in the air. She thinks of her evenings, always the same: homework and dinner and TV, with no thought of outside. And all the while this place existed in the same world. Her brain stretches with the thought of it.

This place is part of the same planet, but like Mum said back in Tromsø, it feels like a different world, a different time. Like Damascus. The bigger the world feels, the more Leila has a sense of panic that she can't be everywhere, do everything. How will she go back to school after a summer spent sledding over sea ice after a blue fox?

They break for lunch on a gentle slope, digging into the softer snow to protect themselves, and the gas fire, from the wind. Leila is surprised how hungry she feels.

'Your brain burns energy, just like any part of your body,' says Matty, smiling as she takes seconds of the soup.

'You did so well, Leila,' says Britt. 'Did they teach you compass reading in school?'

'Kind of,' says Leila, thinking of Box Hill. 'But Matty helped mainly.'

'Yes, very impressive,' says Liv, nudging Mum, who is checking the tracker.

'Hm? Oh, yes. Well done,' says Mum absently. 'Closing in,' she says. 'Lucky it's not one of her hundred-mile days.'

'The captain was right though. We're getting close to Canadian territory,' frowns Liv, scrutinising the screen. 'And you—'

'Not that close,' says Mum.

'Shh!' Matty's voice is urgent.

All four of them look at him in surprise. But it's clear from the expression on Matty's face that he isn't messing around. Leila follows his gaze, over Mum and Liv's heads. She can't see anything, and then there is movement in the distance and Leila's heart turns to ice – the outline, the pebble-black nose of a polar bear.

'Bury the food,' Matty hisses. He is transformed from his usual, loose-limbed stance into someone else, alert and tense, hand steady on the gun though his voice shakes. 'Slow.'

Leila and Britt scrape a shallow bowl into the snow, pouring in the leftover soup, placing the last of the crackers on top. Britt presses snow back over. But it is clear the polar bear has smelt them, seen them. It walks closer with a loping, rolling gait, so much bigger than Leila ever imagined an animal could be. Big as a Range Rover, built as broad, yellow-white fur matted over its hanging belly.

The bear stands now at the base of the slope they sit on. It is nothing like seeing one on television, nothing like a bear from a story. It is unmistakeably, unquestionably *wild*.

Leila has never been so afraid in all her life. In books, when people come face to face with animals, there is some sort of connection, or recognition. But looking at the bear, Leila understands it is just as she'd felt this place was: part of another world. A place where there is nothing between you and starvation except yourself.

She understands that if this bear gets close enough, it will kill them.

But she also understands, by the *click* of Matty's gun, that if it does try to come closer, it will itself be killed.

She doesn't want to see this beautiful, terrifying creature shot just because they are here, and they have brought the smell of food near a hungry animal.

Go, she wills it silently. *Go.*

The bear steps closer. Leila can see the clouds of its breath, brought up boiling from that enormous body, billowing into the cold air.

'If it ducks its head,' Liv whispers.

'I know,' murmurs Matty.

The bear swings its head side to side, sniffing the air. Its neck is thick as a dustbin, its black nose large as Leila's palm. Can it smell the cold sweat prickling over her upper lip? Can it hear her heart, her silent pleas for it to leave?

The bear rears slowly on to its back legs. The snow crunches like gravel beneath its weight. It stands twice as high as any man in the world.

Leila sees the kitchen knife lengths of its claws, the column of its body like a tree rooted in the ice. It seems to be sizing them up, scanning the surroundings, still undecided.

'Spread your arms,' says Matty. 'All of you. Together.'

They flank him, extending like a V of birds, arms outstretched. Leila feels Britt's arms trembling against hers. To the bear, what must they look like? Five terrified humans, or one enormous creature, not worth the fight?

So slowly it is as though time has stopped, the bear drops to all fours again. It steps back, and back again. Finally, it turns, and walks in the direction of the thinner sea ice. None of them talk,

none of them move,
until it is past a speck.
Until it is vanished entirely.

At last, Matty flips the
safety catch, and lowers
his gun.

'Well done,' says Liv
soothingly. Matty collapses,
and Liv wraps her arms around
him as he rocks on his heels.

He takes in a great
shuddering breath. 'I thought
I was going to have
to shoot.'

'He was a male,' says Liv weakly. 'Must have eaten recently. No cubs. We were lucky.'

'If there are bears around, it solves the problem of what she's eating,' says Mum, and Liv makes an impatient sound.

'Still thinking on your fox?'

'Our fox,' says Mum. 'And yes of course. That's why we're here.'

'I don't know if we should carry on,' says Liv. 'With bears so close.'

'We knew there are bears, that's why we have the gun. It's fine,' says Mum.

'It would not be if there had been cubs,' says Liv sternly. 'It would have meant an aggressive mother. These are desperate times for the animals. It's too risky now.'

'It's all a risk!' snaps Mum. 'A calculated one. Look!' She holds up the tracker. 'We are so close. Three more hours, and unless she speeds up, we will see her. Don't you want that too, Liv?'

Leila sees Liv relent. 'I guess. But it should not be up to us. Leila, Britt – are you happy to carry on? Don't look at your Mum,' she adds, blocking Leila's view.

Britt looks uncertain. But Leila, now her shock is leaving her, suddenly wants urgently to keep going. 'I want to carry on. We've come this far.'

'Spoken like a true Saleh,' says Mum proudly.

'Britt?' says Liv. But Leila knows Britt would never show herself to be scared, especially when Leila hasn't.

'Yes,' says Britt. 'We have to keep going.'

This time on the sledge, Leila keeps watch, swivelling her head to take in the entirety of the white landscape. The sun has slunk low to the horizon, creating long blue shadows, and more than once she thinks she sees something moving in the dark, but it is only a trick of brightness and its opposite. A flock of birds flies over them, and Liv calls over her shoulder, 'Terns!' Their cheeping fills the silence, a glorious sign of life.

Leila can't get the bear out of her head. Her fear forgotten, she now feels a mix of wonder and sadness. *Desperate times*. The world is changing so fast, and all animals were suffering – people as well as polar bears and Arctic foxes.

'Here.'

Mum's voice breaks open her thoughts. The bright of night-time is all around them, and they have reached the lip of a shallow basin. Mum unclips herself from the front of the line with trembling fingers, and Leila climbs off the sledge, blood rushing painfully back into her legs. Mum crouches low to the ground, and scrambles to the very edge of the dip. Leila joins her, ducking out of the wind as the others unclips themselves too.

'There.' Mum's voice is barely a breath, and Leila's own catches in her throat.

The basin scoops out below them and there, in a small hollow opposite, is a tiny, curled up shape, like a question mark against the snow.

The fox.

FIFTEEN

The feeling in Leila's chest is almost overwhelming. She'd call it love but that was ridiculous. She can't love a fox, in its own way as wild as that bear had been, this animal she's never met. But there isn't really another word.

Mum is holding the binoculars up to her face in one hand, and with her other grasps Leila's hand tightly. She likes the anchor of it, the rooting, how she feels completely connected to Mum as she looks at the fox, the thing that brought them here.

Mum hands over the binoculars. Barely daring to breathe, Leila holds looks through them, and the fox comes into close and sharp focus. There she is at last – Miso.

She's smaller than a street fox, and where from a distance her fur had looked nearly black, Leila now sees she is indeed blue, the darkest, greyest blue of a smoggy evening. Her face is tucked tight into its tail, draped over itself like a scarf, and as Leila watches she sees a rounded, soft-looking ear twitch in their direction. They duck down, and when Leila next looks through the binoculars, Miso is awake.

Her face is undeniably adorable. Pointed and fluffy, with large, alert, light grey eyes ringed in darker fur, like eyeliner. On her chin is a dab of white she'd never noticed from the photos, like it's been dipped in a bowl of cream. Around her neck is a dark brown collar, with a whisker-thin antenna sticking up from it. The tracker.

Miso sits upright and very still, the wind ruffling her thick fur, her wrapped-around tail as long and thick as her body. Leila is dimly aware that Matty has moved to crouch beside them and is taking photos. It may be her imagination, but Leila thinks she can smell the fox, something warm and musky under the cold cleanness of snow. Miso's head is swivelling,

searching for them,

but they are well hidden by the bluff,

masked by the wind.

She knows they are there though. She doesn't lie back down. She is poised, ready to run. Her sides rise and fall with short, sharp breaths.

The longer they lie there, the more Leila's breath syncs with Miso's, until her head is full of only the fox, the beauty and the sweetness of her, the fear and the curiosity.

Without warning, the wind shifts. Leila feels her hat whip forward over her face, and instinctively she claps a hand over her head to stop it flying off.

'Stop!' hisses Mum, but too late. Miso is running full-pelt up the opposite bank, paws gripping easily on the slick ice, and then, with a flash of blue-grey tail, she is gone. Matty lets out a long breath and checks his camera display.

'Al'ama,' says Mum. 'You scared her!'

'That isn't fair, Amani,' says Liv. 'The wind changed. She smelt us.'

'And we got loads of photos,' says Matty, turning the display to face them. Leila sees a close-up of Miso's face. 'Perfect for Twitter, yes?'

She tries to return Matty's smile, but Mum's blame has stung her. The calm she'd felt watching the fox has evaporated.

'Let's get after her,' says Mum, but Liv shakes her head.

'It's midnight,' she says. 'We'll pitch up here for the night. She'll be running for a while now. We can catch her up tomorrow.'

Mum looks like she will argue, but a sudden yawn stretches her mouth. She looks as surprised as Liv, and laughs. 'I guess my body agrees with you.'

Her mood has lightened, and she smiles at Leila. 'It wasn't your fault. Can you see why I'm obsessed though?'

'Yes,' says Leila, honestly. 'She's so small! I didn't expect her to be that small.'

'So small,' agrees Mum. 'And she's walked nearly two thousand miles. Two thousand! We've skied fifty today. Can you believe it?'

'She looked well fed,' says Liv. 'And the ice here is too thick for her to fish. So there must be more bears around.'

'Liv,' Mum sounds exasperated. 'We know there are bears. That's what the gun is for. I'll take first watch while you get some sleep.'

'Looking at you I think I should take first watch,' says Liv.

'No offence, Mum,' says Leila, pointing at the bags under Mum's eyes, 'but she's right.'

While Matty and Liv sit outside with the gun in the bright night, Leila lies down between Britt and Mum, her head spinning with everything she has seen and felt since they've started out across the ice. She pins her thoughts in place, like the map on Mum's research wall.

She knows where they are from her navigation: International Waters, just below Greenland. On one of their late-night fishing excursions, she'd asked Lenny about how the sea borders worked.

'It's not like you can draw a line across the sea,' she'd said.

'You can,' confirmed Lenny. 'That's exactly what they did to the land. My family are Sámi—'

'You don't look Sámi,' interrupted Britt.

Lenny frowned. 'What do you expect us to look like?'

Britt flushed. 'I only mean—'

'I know what you meant,' said Lenny. 'My mother is part-Norwegian. But her father was Sámi, and so is mine, and hundreds of years ago what we call north Norway and Finland and Sweden and part of Russia was one place, Sápmi.'

'Across the top?' asked Leila. 'Like Lapland?'

Lenny's face darkened further. 'That is not a good word, Lapp. It's the word we were given, not the one we chose.'

'Sorry,' said Leila hurriedly. She understood this. Amma had said similar, when people called them names, even ones that didn't seem that offensive. *It makes us other*, she says. *Same as when they call us migrants when we come here, and themselves expats when they go elsewhere. Like they have some ownership. Like they belong in a way we can't.*

'Sápmi, yes?' Britt asked eagerly, trying to make amends.

'Yes.'

'It belonged to you? Your ancestors, I mean?'

Lenny laughed, but not unkindly. 'Belonged, no. We lived there, travelled across forests in winter, Arctic tundras in summer, following reindeer. Slowly, the lines were drawn, and we could go places less and less. Sea borders are very real. It's part of the reason we thought hard about this charter, though of course I disagree there should ever be such restrictions.'

'Why did that matter to this charter?' asked Leila, and Lenny had given her an odd, almost pitying look.

'Rules,' he shrugged. Norwegians had a whole language of shrugs, like the way Mona's eyebrows could speak full sentences.

Leila had wanted to push, but Britt was already climbing down to the boat. Now, sandwiched between her sleeping friend and mother, she remembers Lenny's words about drawing lines across the sea, and thinks about the little blue fox, cutting her own path across them all.

Leila wakes and sees Liv lying the other side of Britt. They are cuddled into each other, Liv's watch illuminated in the dark canvas tent. 6:04.

She'd never wake up so early at home, but here her sleep feels deeper and more complete. She pulls on her coat, hat, gloves and boots, and wriggles out from the tent as quietly as she can.

Mum and Matty are sitting outside, talking softly, the gun in the crook of Mum's arm. The gas stove is lit in front of them, coffee on the boil in the small pan, and the laptop stands open on a little tray, its screen glowing softly. Mum sees her and smiles, her eyes tired but face bright and more relaxed than Leila's seen it in days. Miso has made her happy.

'Morning La-La. Hot chocolate?'

Leila nods while Matty yawns and stretches. 'I'm going to sleep an hour.'

'Fine,' says Mum, rummaging through a pack. He disappears into a separate tent, zipping it closed behind. 'We thought it was fine to risk coffee. Not usually part of a polar bear's diet. Enti bkhair?'

'Fine,' says Leila, determinedly answering in English. Hearing her mum speak Arabic still feels like a punch to the gut.

Mum looks at her long and hard before deciding not to react.

'Surely more than fine, after seeing her?'

Despite herself, Leila returns Mum's smile. 'Yeah.'

Mum breathes in deeply, looking around at the white expanse. 'You can see why people love the Arctic. All this blankness, waiting to be explored. But of course, it isn't blank, not really. So much life, all around us.' Mum pats the ice with a gloved hand. 'Just think. Right now, under us there is a whole world of narwhales and seals and fish. Doesn't it blow your mind?'

It actually makes Leila a bit queasy. Mum frowns at her.

'Are you all right really, Leila? I know this is probably not what you had in mind for your summer.'

'That's an understatement.'

Mum snorts and pours Leila's hot chocolate into a mug. 'Matty uploaded the photos on to here.' She taps the sturdy laptop with its dongle that connects them to a satellite in space. 'He said to pick one and tweet it.'

Leila sips her warm, sugary drink and thinks of Mona, how

she always makes Leila hot chocolate after dinner. She takes a deep breath. 'Can we call Amma and Mona soon?'

Mum hesitates, but then smiles. 'Of course. How about now?'

The number is so familiar it almost transports Leila back to some sort of recognisable reality. She presses the satellite phone to her ear and feels something close to elation when Amma answers.

'Hello? Who is it?' She sounds panicked, and Leila suddenly realises the time. It's even earlier in London. She winces. 'Amma?'

'Leila?' Amma's voice rises a few notches. 'What is it, habibti? Are you OK?'

'I'm fine, Amma, fine.'

Leila can hear Mona talking shrilly in the background, and the familiar click as she puts her on loudspeaker. 'Leila? What is it? Where are you?'

'I'm fine,' repeats Leila, her own panic rising to meet theirs. 'I lost track of time.'

'Lost track?' Mona's voice is incredulous. 'Why are you calling now? Why haven't you called? You said you'd call every day!'

'I didn't—'

'I want the number,' says Mona.

Mum is chewing her nail, nervously. She can't give her away.

'I'm calling from a telephone box,' she says. 'The phone in Mum's apartment is down.'

Amma sucks her teeth audibly.

'You're lying,' says Mona, and there is shock in her voice. 'Where's your mum? Let me speak to her.'

Leila holds the phone out dumbly, and Mum takes it, worry clear across her face. As she speaks, Leila can hear the rapid replies on the end of the line.

'Hello. Yes, she's fine. No, honestly. We've just been busy.' Mum chews her nail again. 'Not now. Soon. Let me speak to your Mum. Zaha? It's all right, I promise. I know it's too early. The midnight sun . . . Yes . . . Yes of course. Here.'

Leila takes the phone back, her hands are shaking slightly. Mona speaks over Amma. 'Leila, you're going to FaceTime us later, OK? You've got to promise.'

'Promise,' says Leila miserably.

'Good. I'm going back to sleep. I swear, if you come back a morning person, I'll kill you.'

Leila hangs up the phone, which feels heavy as a brick in her hand. Heavy as her heart in her chest.

The panic was in her like a poison. She'd walked and walked, and finally smelt nothing. She found a soft place, a high place, a safe place, but when she woke, their smell was back. She heard their noises, unnatural snaps like teeth.

Fox is running now.
She must not be caught again.

She runs and runs, finding leavings of bears,
enough not to starve.

When she is not eating, she is running.

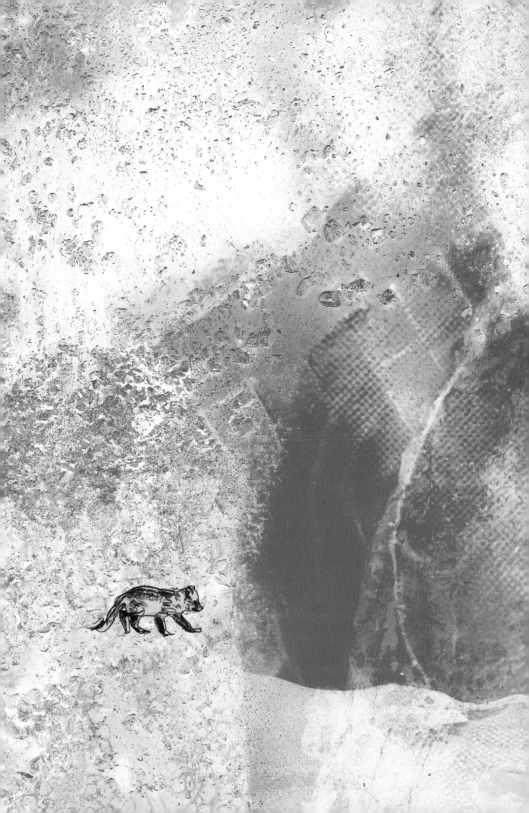

The sea   is breaking

its pane of ice.

Her paw smashes through thin ice, and she is up to her chest,
her belly soaked.

She is in the water, and her fur
is dragging her down.

Below, a pod of orcas pass, not interested for now.

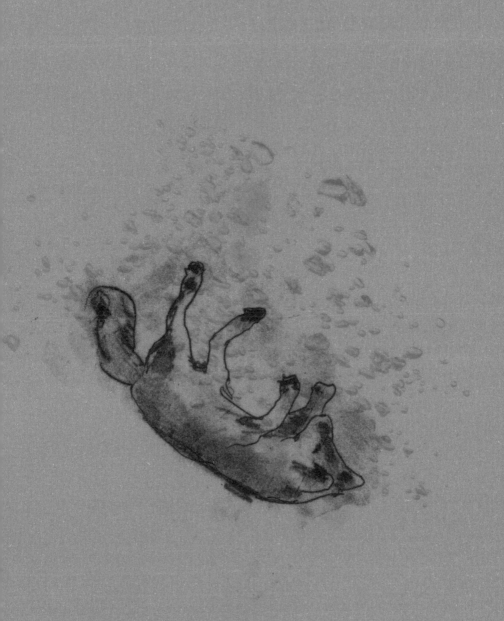

Her scrabbling claws find purchase,
she heaves herself up.
It takes all her strength.

She lies panting on the floe, her fur already freezing to icicles, her body small as a cat's.

She is very tired. She hides her soft face in her soft paws. A blizzard comes, and covers her like a blanket.

Fox cannot move.

Fox stays.

SIXTEEN

The plain before them is like a sheet of paper. It's like Mum said – a whole blank space unrolling, but it has already been explored by countless animals and some people. As they start to cross this, the final sea border before Canada, Leila sees it is actually nothing like a sheet of paper.

Instead, it is like sand seen under a microscope. What seemed like uniform grains was suddenly revealed as tiny fragments of eroded shells, vibrant with colour and variety. The same is true here: up close the ice is snarled and wrinkled, full of deep drops and short, sharp slopes, its colours blue and grey and green.

Shortly after she'd selected a photo – Miso looking straight at the camera, rounded ears cocked and eyes wide – and uploaded the tweet saying they'd seen her and that she'd now walked over two thousand miles, Leila checked the tracker, and she reported Miso had walked another thirty miles overnight, crossing into Canadian territories, and seemed to be resting on one spot.

'Excellent work, navigator! We can catch her up again,' said Mum excitedly.

'She's headed off the sea ice,' said Leila.

'On to land?' asked Liv, and all Leila could hear in her voice was worry. 'There's plenty of research about foxes on land.'

'So we better catch her before she reaches it,' said Mum, and there was warning in her voice. She'd radioed to tell the boat their location and plan. Captain Johansson had sounded worried too.

'We're free of the ice. We can come and collect you, could be there in two hours.'

'We're happy crossing by skis.'

'When we cross over the border, we'll have to disclose our reasons to the coastguard,' he said. 'You understand?'

Mum said she did, but Leila certainly didn't. All the grown-ups seemed cagey today, but thoughts of it soon faded as they left the powdered snow of the basin behind and set out over the glittering ice.

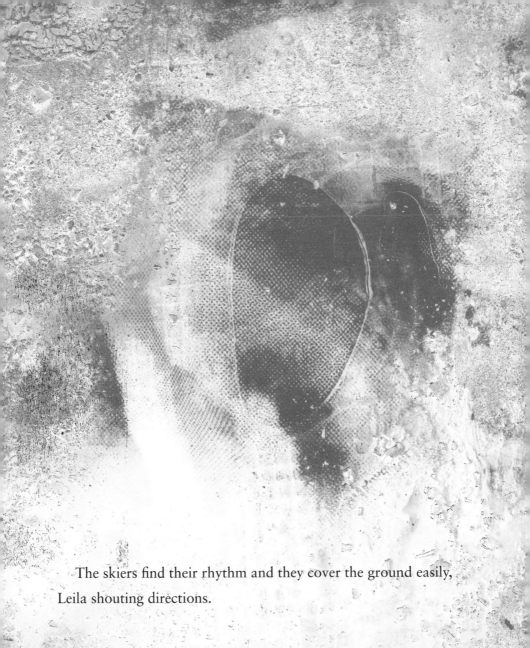

The skiers find their rhythm and they cover the ground easily,
Leila shouting directions.

Suddenly, they draw up short, Mum's cry an alarm cutting through the wind.

Leila stares around them, heart hammering, expecting to see a bear. But all she can see beyond them is . . . She blinks. It doesn't immediately make sense. In front of them the icy plain seems to be viewed through a kaleidoscope, the pieces jumbled into a new order.

The sea ice is breaking up. Closest to them, it seems almost solid, but is bobbing gently, imperceptible as breath, on the rhythm of the waves.

Further out, perhaps ten feet, it breaks up entirely into shimmering discs of blue-white. Then come the gaps filled with the grey sea, more floating patches of ice, and even further away is—

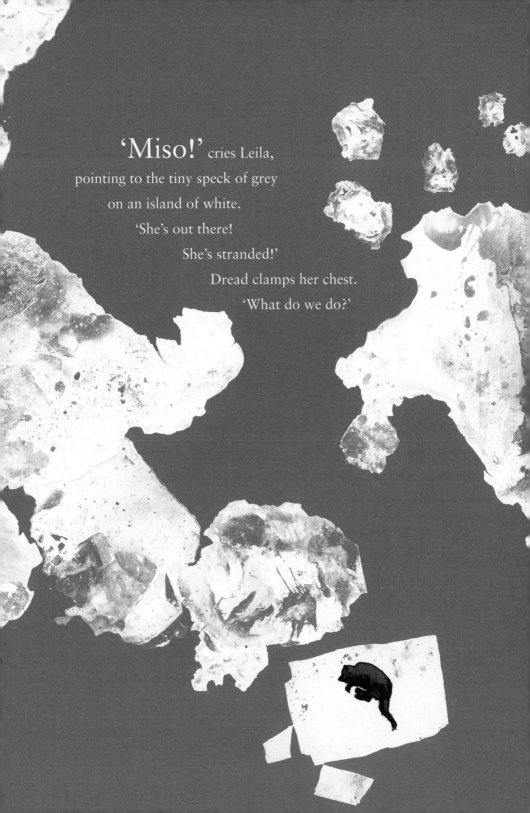

'Miso!' cries Leila,
pointing to the tiny speck of grey
on an island of white.
'She's out there!
She's stranded!'
Dread clamps her chest.
'What do we do?'

'Nothing,' says Liv.

Mum turns to Liv, yanking her snow goggles off her face, her eyes furious. 'You can't be serious.'

Liv's face is strained but resolute. 'This is the way, Amani. I told you it might go like this. Whatever happens next, we can only watch.'

Britt makes a choking sound, forcing out her words. 'Mamma, *nei*.'

'This is not a film, Britt,' says Liv. 'The ice is too unstable, she is too far out. It's not our job to interfere.'

'But you already have!' says Leila, losing her temper with the force of a lightning bolt. 'You caged her, tracked her. We've chased her all this way—'

'You're saying this is my fault?' says Mum wildly, rounding on Leila.

'No, I'm saying you've already interfered, so why can't we save her?'

'I agree, Leila,' says Matty in a sad, soothing voice. 'But Liv is right. We can't get to her.'

They turn to look at Miso, the tiny fox stuck on the drifting ice. She has moved further away from their diminishing coast, is splayed flat against the slippery surface. Leila's breath quickens, as though she feels the fox's fear, its confusion. Her eyes fill with tears.

'We can't just leave her.' Leila lets out a muffled sort of cry. 'We can call the captain. What did he say? Two hours?'

'That was hours ago,' says Liv. 'He might be docked by now.'

But Mum is looking at Leila, with a fierce pride in her eyes. 'He can come back. We'll reach her by boat.'

Liv opens her mouth to argue, but the sight of Britt and Leila's stricken faces seem to sway her. She shakes her head exasperatedly, and gestures for Matty to unpack the satellite phone.

It is the longest few hours of Leila's life. Mum and Matty take turns watching Miso's iceberg through the binoculars while Liv paces agitatedly, snapping at them all to get back from the edge. Leila tells herself to breathe deeply and slowly, pulling her thoughts away from Miso again and again.

At long last, they hear a sound that is not the ice shifting or the sea murmuring or the wind blowing.

'The boat,' says Mum, voice cracking. 'Alhamdulillah.'

'Alhamdulillah,' repeats Leila.

The Floe powers into view, making the already-drifting ice bob and break apart further. Captain Johansson sends out the small boat to collect them.

Lenny's face is more serious than Leila has ever seen it as he helps them load their bags and then themselves into the vessel, and he is silent on the short journey back to the ship, despite Britt's greeting. Once they've ascended the metal ladder to the deck, Captain Johansson intercepts them.

'Wheelhouse,' says Captain Johansson, without so much as a hello. 'Now.'

Mum motions for Britt and Leila to stay on deck, but they crouch down behind the ice boxes, and edge as close as they can.

'This is beyond my remit,' says Captain Johansson. 'It is not safe, and more than that—'

'We are paying you,' says Mum.

'Yes, but you do not own us. There are only so many risks—'

'Please,' says Mum. 'We only need to see her safe. I'll take full responsibility—'

'Only the captain has full responsibility on a boat.'

'Then put me back on the ice when we're close enough.'

Leila clenches her fist at Mum's words. They are exactly what she would have said, how she feels.

'You know that's not an option. We've permission to be here in Baffin Bay, but—'

'What's going on?' whispers Britt. 'What does the captain mean?'

'I don't know.'

The wheelhouse door slams shut, and they can no longer hear what's being said.

They wait nervously, until finally the door opens. Mum strides out, looking triumphant. 'We're going after Miso,' she says.

Matty trails after her, looking miserable.

'What's up with him?' says Britt. 'Isn't this what he wanted too?'

'Only Amani is getting what she wants,' says Liv darkly. 'And it's certainly not what's right for her.'

Leila frowns and follows after Mum and Matty, down the familiar metal steps. It feels strange to be back aboard this cramped dark boat after the expanse of light and whiteness, claustrophobic. She enters the familiar map-strewn room. Mum looks round at her.

'Why is Captain Johansson so worried about you going after the fox?' asks Leila.

'No idea,' says Mum lightly. 'But he's agreed, and that's all that matters. Plus, we've got some good news, haven't we Matty?'

Matty grins weakly, and turns the laptop to face Leila, and there is the tweet Leila sent from the Arctic plain:

Miso has now walked 2,600 miles, and today we watched her sleeping in the snow for a while, until she saw us. She seems healthy and happy, and she says hello! Next stop, Canada. Click the link in our bio for where she's been, and follow #WhereIsMiso for photographs and updates.

The photo looks even better large on the laptop screen. You can see the lustrous texture of Miso's deep blue fur, the golden flecks in her eyes. She can't bear the thought of her out on the sea, trapped on a melting float of ice.

Mum taps the icon below the tweet. Leila frowns at it, then feels her jaw drop.

3.3k retweets 12.5k likes

As she watches, it ticks up a few more numbers.

'We're infectious!' says Mum.

'Viral,' corrects Matty.

'National Geographic retweeted us a minute ago. And we're getting loads of traffic to the website, aren't we Matty?'

He confirms with a tight nod. He still seems miserable, and it dampens Leila's excitement.

'We should direct them to some sort of funding page,' says Leila. 'Can we add a donation link?'

'Excellent idea,' says Mum. 'We should show Captain Johansson, so he understands it's not just us who care. All these people do too.'

Mum chatters on, and maybe it is only because she's worrying about Miso, but Leila thinks maybe she doesn't want to leave a silence long enough for Leila to ask what's wrong, and Matty to tell her.

She has never been so cold, never had water soak so deep through her fur before, so close to her skin. She curls herself as tightly as she can, tight as she was once tucked inside her mother's belly alongside her brothers and sisters. She cannot remember their warmth now, but she feels the lack of it.

There is sea all around, and she understands there is sea also below her, through the ice that nibbles her paws. She is very hungry, very weak. She must not sleep.

She keeps one eye open, above her quivering tail.

Fox does not know to hope,
but she waits for something to change,

or else for nothing.

SEVENTEEN

Even to Leila's untrained eye, she can tell the water is treacherous. Icebergs of varying sizes drift past the hull, sometimes rising almost high as the deck.

Captain Johansson stands by Lenny's shoulder in the wheelhouse, jaw set, focussed only on steering them to safety. Britt and Leila join the rest of the crew in looking over the sides, calling out when they spot an especially large or jagged ice floe. At the same time, they are constantly scanning for the Miso, knowing she is close by but so hard to spot, a tiny speck on a vanishing raft.

The call comes in the early evening. Britt leans over the railing, and shouts joyfully. 'There! She's there!'

Leila almost trips in her haste to see, banging hard into the railing, the breath knocked from her. There, only fifty feet away, a small circle of white bobs in the mercifully still sea. At its centre, like a bullseye, is a tiny, blue-grey shape. Even from this distance, Leila can see Miso is trembling. Her heart aches. She wants to leap into the water and swim to her as fast as possible.

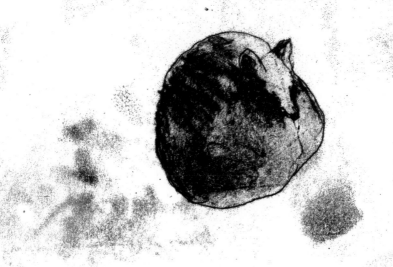

'Quick,' says Mum. 'The landing boat.'

Liv, Matty and Britt stay on board *The Floe*, reluctantly agreeing that they need space and stillness in the boat when approaching Miso. Mum takes charge of the dart gun, and alongside, Leila boards the landing craft with Lenny, the large wire cage slotted between their legs.

It takes them barely two minutes to reach Miso, but it feels far longer. The fox sees them coming and uncurls. She trembles harder, edging right to the furthest point of the sliver of ice, and beginning to pace. Leila has nightmarish visions of her falling into the freezing sea, drowning before any of them can reach her.

At last, they draw up alongside the ice floe, which is now about the size of a school gym mat. Lenny cuts the engine, and they regard each other, fox and humans, with a reflected desperation.

Mum's eyes are bright as she lifts the small gun to her cheek.

'What are you doing?' hisses Leila, horrified.

'It's just a dart. We need to sedate her,' says Mum. 'It won't hurt her, just put her to sleep so we can get her off the iceberg. We only have one shot.'

Leila swallows drily. She closes her eyes and holds her breath as she hears Mum pull the trigger. She breathes out and opens her eyes.

Miso is lying limply at the centre of the iceberg, her breaths deep and steady, the dart red against her dark fur.

'Nice shot,' says Lenny. The boat nudges the iceberg, and a chunk of ice splits off. 'Now, who is fetching her?'

'Me of course,' says Mum, already reaching for the cage.

'That berg is about to break,' says Lenny, 'the best chance is for the lightest person to go. He looks at Leila.

Leila doesn't even have to think. She stands and swings her leg over the side of the boat, her feet land on the iceberg.

'Leila!' Mum's hands clamp over her coat. 'You need a rope at least!'

'There's no time! I can do this. Trust me.'

Mum hesitates, but Leila eases herself free from her grasp.

'Lie flat across the ice, OK?' says Mum. 'It'll spread your weight.'

Leila nods, forcing herself not to think too hard. Mum and Lenny hold her under the arms, taking her weight as she slowly lowers her body on to the ice. It dips slightly, water slopping over the slick surface and finding a gap in her coat, making her gasp in discomfort.

'Stay still,' says Mum. 'Find your balance.'

Leila's eyes fix on the small, furred shape only an arm's length away. She wants to lunge for the fox, be out of this situation as quickly as possible, but she knows if she rushes, she'll tip them both into the sea.

Slowly, the berg stops rocking. Leila stretches out
her arm, sliding her opposite leg up underneath
her body. This low to the ocean, the
water feels far rougher, the
chill coming off it
like steam,

its fathomless depths taking on storybook proportions.

Leila pulls with her arm and pushes with her leg. She breathes shallowly, feels the berg shift as her body disrupts its balance, letting more water wash over it. She hears herself gasp and tries to focus only on her breath.

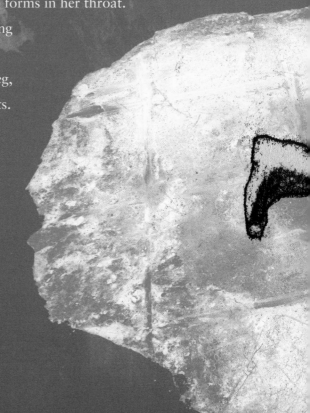

She slithers slowly closer and places her gloved hand on Miso's gently rising ribcage. Her hand sinks into the deep fur, disappearing, and even through the gloves Leila feels the bright shock of her warmth, sparking along her arm to her heart.

She half expects the fox to wake and bite her, but the dart has done its job. She finds deeper purchase with her foot and pushes closer. Her hand scoops under Miso's ribs. She is lighter than Leila expected. A lump forms in her throat.

Then a deep rumbling

crack

vibrates along her leg,

and the ice splits.

'Leila!'

Mum cries out, and Leila throws herself forwards to grip the small creature with both hands as she feels herself start to slide backwards, water soaking over the top of her boots, so cold it scalds her skin. Her brain stops, her body stops. All she can think of is Miso, keeping her safe.

She draws her tight against her chest
as she skids into the water.

In a confusion of hands, on her legs, her arms, her shoulders, her hair, she is pulled from the sea and tumbled into the base of the boat. Her head strikes the hard plastic seat, but she feels the pain far away.

She will not let them take Miso from her. As the boat's engine starts up and she is bundled inside Matty's coat, all she feels is Miso's heartbeat against her own, her fur against the bare skin of Leila's wrist, all she smells is the sharp, cold scent of the fox, all she knows is Miso is safe and in her arms, and she never wants to let go.

Liv insists Miso must wake up somewhere wild.

'We can't keep her like a pet, even for a day,' she says. Captain Johansson has called another emergency summit in his wheelhouse, and this time Leila and Britt are allowed in too, Leila in clean, dry clothes with a mug of hot chocolate in her hands. Mum is keeping a tight hold of her.

Leila knows what she did was dangerous, and could have ended differently, but she doesn't care. All she cares about is that Miso is safely on board, a towel draped over her cage in case the sedation wears off early and she panics. Leila had imagined more time with her, seeing those gold-flecked eyes fixed on hers, a spark of understanding that it was Leila who rescued her. But Liv is right. It is not how it should be.

'Where is the nearest land?' asks Liv.

'Hans Island is only two miles away,' says Captain Johansson. 'But it is disputed.' Leila doesn't understand what he means.

'We'll go there,' says Liv, firmly. 'All right, Amani? We'll leave her on the island, and then we're going home.'

'Not yet, it's too fast! If I could just—' Mum begins to protest.

But Liv talks over her. 'We've done what we set out to do. More than. We've recorded the longest, fastest journey an Arctic fox has ever made. We've seen how she scavenges for food, how friable the sea ice is. We can prove all the things we need to prove, make the arguments we need to make. You've risked enough.

Leila's risked enough. We all have.'

Mum looks at Leila, at her pale lips, and sighs, pulling her closer. 'You're right.'

But Leila doesn't want to be the reason it's all over. 'I did it because I wanted to. Because I care about Miso too.'

'This isn't just about one fox!' snaps Liv. 'It never was. It's about why animals have to leave their habitats and seek new ones. It's about how they do it. If they even can – and Miso has shown how adaptable they can be.'

'But National Geographic retweeted us—' says Leila.

'Twitter is not real life, Leila,' says Liv severely. All her usually amiability is gone. 'It doesn't matter what people "like" or "retweet". It's about what they *do*.'

'We've raised eight thousand euros for the institute since yesterday,' says Matty quietly.

'Not you too,' sighs Liv.

'Leila's right to care,' insists Matty. 'This sort of engagement, it can only be good. People need stories.'

'Stories?' says Liv, exasperated.

'Things to care about,' says Leila, shrugging off Mum's arm and standing next to Matty. 'Miso is that for every person who gave money or wanted to. So what if she is only one fox? Isn't it better we saved her today than not?'

'Sometimes we need stories just as much, if not more, than

shelter,' adds Mum. 'More than food.'

Liv's face softens. 'Yes, of course. I love stories as much as anyone. But I am a scientist, and I'm your friend, Amani. I have a responsibility. We leave her on Hans Island. That story is done. Miso doesn't belong to us. She belongs to the land, and the sea, and to herself.'

At long last, Mum nods. Leila sets down her hot chocolate and pulls on Mum's hand. 'Come on. We have two miles.'

She leads Mum to the darkened room where Miso still sleeps, her pink tongue peeking from between her slack jaws. Leila thinks about opening the cage, holding her warm, lovely weight against her chest again, but now it seems wrong. Miso is wild, and that is why she is so wonderful. That is why they have to let her go.

'Enti bkhair, Mama?'

Mum looks at her with such delight and surprise and sadness, Leila thinks she might start crying. Mum's eyes are filling with tears already.

'I'm OK, La-La. You?'

'Same.'

Leila snuggles into her mum's side. It is all still there – the hurt and the unanswered questions and the fear of what will happen next. But right now, Leila is happy to be quiet and still in this dark room, the snuffling breaths of a sleeping fox, the smell of rosewater in the air.

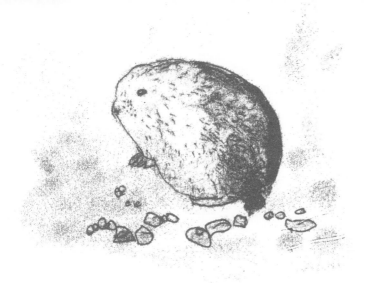

EIGHTEEN

Hans Island is a tiny hump of thawing land surrounded by thick, locked ice. To its west, the coast of Canada's Ellesmere Island rises. To the east, Greenland. It feels to Leila like an in-between place, a crossing point, and a perfect place for Miso to decide whether to stay, return, or carry on across the sea ice.

The boat gets within a hundred feet of the island's shore before the ice thickens too much to progress further.

'We can't leave her on the ice,' says Matty.

'Matty and I will take her to land,' says Liv, and Mum looks at her with eyes so defiant it makes Leila gulp.

'We are all going, or no one is going,' says Mum, with no hint of compromise in her voice.

'You mustn't—' starts Liv.

'Please,' snaps Mum. 'Not now.'

And so it is that Liv, Britt, Matty and Leila find themselves strapping on snowshoes, and following Mum and a sleeping, caged fox, out on to the ice once more. Leila is glad they don't need to ski, that she can walk on her own two feet to complete this final task for Miso. They walk in silence, like a funeral procession, heads downcast.

Leila knows she should feel happy, glad that Miso will be safely left with all her choices her own. But she feels only a great sadness that soon it will be over. She is not ready to leave the Arctic just yet.

When they reach land, Leila looks up. Hans Island is domed like a mosque, and everywhere the snow is not, are wildflowers. Thousands and thousands of flowers, in red, blue, green, yellow and pink. Britt laughs with delight.

'It's beautiful!'

'It's summer,' murmurs Liv. 'Miso walked a whole season.'

Mum sets down the cage and hugs Liv. The women hold each other tightly, and Leila can tell by Liv's shaking shoulders she is crying. Mum's eyes are also full of tears as she draws back and pulls Matty into the hug.

Leila tugs the camera from Matty's abandoned rucksack and takes a picture of the hugging scientists, the cage with its sleeping, sweet-faced fox, framed against the riot of the flowered hillside.

Britt slings an arm across Leila's shoulders and rolls her eyes. 'So soft, these scientists.' But Leila sees her eyes are bright too.

'OK,' says Mum briskly. 'Time to say goodbye.'

Liv bends down to the cage. *'Farvel lille rev.* You walked all this way. You are a marvel. Thank you for showing us more wonder than we ever hoped to find.'

'*Farvel,*' says Matty. 'Thanks for all the data! And look.' He points at several small burrowed mounds of earth amongst the flowers. 'Lemmings. She will be well fed here.'

Mum nods, biting her lip bravely.

'Bye, little fox,' says Britt, her voice catching.

Leila crouches down beside the cage. The fox's fur riffles in the breeze. Her whiskers twitch. 'Bye Miso,' she whispers, voice breaking.

Mum squeezes her shoulder. 'You take her.'

Leila blinks dumbly, not understanding.

'Of course it must be you,' says Liv. 'You rescued her from the ice, after all.'

'And got all those donations for the institute,' says Matty. 'Go on Leila, you let her go.'

Leila doesn't trust herself to speak. She only nods. Matty lifts

204

the cage into her arms.

'Find somewhere raised up, but with access to the sea. Somewhere she can shelter from the wind,' advises Liv.

'You'll find the perfect place,' smiles Mum. 'You'll know it when you see it.'

Leila's arms encase the cage, stretched wide around its precious cargo. She turns her back on them and begins to walk.

She follows the curve of the island, a gentle incline rising away from the frozen sea to the west. The view becomes more and more beautiful the higher she carries the cage, the flowers like a patchwork. The wind drops here, sheltered by the rocks rising overhead, and she can hear Miso's snuffling breaths, still deep from the sedative. She must leave her somewhere safe, somewhere lovely.

Finally, Leila spots a pebble beach, like the one she'd seen in the very first photo of Miso. She climbs down the slope a little, towards the sea. As she walks through the flowers, she sees small scurrying creatures scattering around her. Lemmings. Lots for Miso to catch, to grow her strong.

Leila reaches a lip of rock, an outcrop with a natural hollow in it. She sets the cage down, and sits beside it, the flowers smelling strong and bright. She inhales deeply, in and out, savouring the smells, the sight. From here, Miso will wake and see Ellesmere Island, Canada, a whole continent from where she began.

Leila unlatches the cage and reaches inside. She scoops the fox gently from the cage, softly, as she would a sleeping cat. Miso sighs, exhaling with a squeaky sound so sweet it sets Leila's teeth on edge. She holds her, briefly, to her chest, feeling the fox's heartbeat once more against hers. She breathes deeper, inhaling the sharp smell of fox, feeling thick fur against her neck.

'Here we are, Miso.' Leila forces herself to let go, placing Miso down gently in the shelter of the rocky hollow. Miso is still sleeping, but her breath is shallower now as she rises from the sedative, her dab-of-cream chin twitching. Leila hesitates a moment, then reaches for the collar.

Her gloves are too thick, and she pulls them off, cold air nibbling her fingertips. Her hands sink into the soft fur as she unlatches the collar. They might as well do it properly: letting her go. She wants to bury her face in Miso's fur, like she used to with Basbousa. But instead she leans down low, to whisper in the fox's soft, hooded ear.

'I won't forget you.

But I hope you forget me.'

Tears prickling hot in her eyes, she stands, and walks back the way she came. Before she rounds the hump of the hill, she looks back. From this distance, she can only just make out the small shape of Miso, but if you didn't know where to look, she would be perfectly invisible. As though she was never there at all. *Or rather*, thinks Leila, *as though it is exactly where she should be.*

NINETEEN

As soon as they arrive back on board, Leila tweets the final photo of Miso on the beach.

Mission Miso complete. This little fox walked 2,700 miles, the furthest and fastest ever recorded. Now we're going to leave her to continue her journey in peace. But if you care about Miso, please learn how you can help save her habitat and donate here #WhereIsMiso

The moment she posts it, the numbers start racking up. Their account has three thousand followers now, and it rises every minute she watches. Leila hesitates a moment, then adds another tweet to the thread.

Here are the scientists who recorded her incredible journey. They're working hard to save the Arctic and all who live there. They're real-life heroes: Professor Amani Saleh, Dr Liv Nilsen, Mathew Willumsen. Read more about them and their research here: bit.ly/arcticinstitute #WhereIsMiso

She attaches the photo of them hugging on Hans Island, tagging the location. It's a good photo, even if she says so herself, the colours rich and bright, the circle of scientists echoing the curled-up Miso in her cage.

'A little melodramatic,' says Matty, smiling. 'But I love it.'

That night, all the adults except Mum drink small thimbles of sharp smelling liquor and Lenny brings a guitar on deck and Captain Johansson sings and Liv and Mum dance and it is altogether too embarrassing for Leila and Britt. They escape to the landing craft, neither of them in the mood to fish but both happy to sit there together on the bobbing waves, facing Canada.

'Have you ever been?' asks Britt.

'No. Never been anywhere before here. Except Damascus.' Damascus, and all the places they had to pass through to get to the UK. Leila imagines a map, the route they took by foot, by car, by boat – she swallows. Her view of the journey is no longer safely at a distance. She sees dark roads, dark hills, a dark sea. She trembles. Suddenly, the memory taps again, and knocks a bit harder: the rock of the boat matches another, from a long time ago.

'Do you miss Damascus?'

With relief, Leila feels Britt's voice pull her back. If she'd asked her a month ago, Leila could have answered *no* without hesitation. But being here with Mum, being reminded of how big the world is, makes her feel differently.

'It's home,' she says. 'It's where Mum and I lived. I miss that. But I love London. I'm happy living with Amma and Mona. I don't think if I could snap my fingers, I'd go back to everything how it used to be.'

'I get what you mean,' says Britt. 'I feel the same about when my parents were together, the house we lived in. You miss the time as much as you miss the place.'

'Exactly! Like obviously I hate that there's war. I hate that we had to leave. But I love that Amma and Mona made me a home.' Leila has never talked like this before, but it feels easy now, after all the impossible things she's seen and done. 'Even though some people don't want us to live there, we do. It's our home, too. One of them.'

'It's tough, not being able to go back.'

'Yeah,' says Leila, and she doesn't only mean Damascus. She

means back to Mum living with her, walking in the heat to the shops, parties on the rooftop, to before the war.

'What's that?' says Britt sharply.

Leila peers out at the sea. In the distance is a boat, bigger than *The Floe*. It appears to be coming straight towards them, fast.

'Are there pirates in the Arctic?' Britt means it as a joke, but Leila has a funny feeling in her belly. She leaps up and starts climbing the ladder.

The grown-ups are all gathered in the prow of the boat, singing raucously. Leila threads through the merriment to Mum, who is singing louder than anyone. Leila tugs her sleeve, and Mum whoops and pulls her into her side.

'There's a boat,' says Leila urgently.

'Indeed,' Mum says, over the tuneless roars of the others. 'We are on one.'

'A boat, coming from over there. It looks— I don't like it.'

Mum's grin falters. 'What do you mean?'

'There's a boat, coming really fast towards us.'

Mum lets Leila lead her through the singing crew to the railing. The boat is much closer now, close enough to make out a red and white flag fluttering from a short mast. Mum's expression changes completely. She grips Captain Johansson's wrist. The captain, thinking she is still joining in, play-acts struggling to be free.

'Let him go! We will not let him go!'

'Coastguard,' she says, and the word cuts through the air like a knife. Lenny drops the guitar with a discordant *clang*.

'Below deck,' says Captain Johansson.

Mum's eyes are wild. 'What about Leila—'

'She's not logged,' says Captain Johansson, a grimace on his face. 'You never registered her. They won't know.'

'Thank you,' says Mum, hand on her heart. Captain Johansson gives a tight nod.

'Below deck,' he repeats. 'Now.'

The adults scatter, crew spread across the deck, hiding the empty bottles. Leila is confused. Surely a coastguard wouldn't care about drinks? Mum is pulling her towards the metal staircase, down into the belly of the ship. Leila looks over her shoulder. She doesn't understand why everyone isn't following them.

'It'll be fine,' says Mum, shoving Leila into the bunkroom. 'You don't have to worry. Just be quiet if they come aboard.'

Mum locks the door behind them. Leila's tummy is churning. Something is dawning on her, with slow-motion horror.

'Mum?' she starts, but Mum hushes her. She turns out the light.

They can hear nothing of what's happening on deck. Leila's mouth is full of questions, but she's worried she already knows the answers. Lenny's strange comments, Liv's worried outbursts, Captain Johansson's reluctance.

It feels like they are in the dark for ever. Mum is sitting next to Leila on the bed, her arms around her. She is trying to appear calm, but Leila can feel her trembling, like Miso on the iceberg, feeling safe ground melt from beneath her.

Footsteps on the metal stairs.
Hard, aggressive steps.
Voices.
Liv's slightly shrill,
Matty's even more so.

Without warning, Mum pushes Leila flat,
yanks the blanket up over her.

'They don't know you are here,' she says. 'Don't move.'

'Mum—' Leila grasps for her hand, but Mum has already moved out of reach, and is unlocking the door.

The room floods briefly with light, and she hears Mum say,
'It's all right. I'm here,' before the door clangs closed,

plunging Leila

once more

into the dark.

Foxes do dream. Here is Fox's.

The sky dusty with stars. The wind strong and blowing. Her belly full and she is running. Above her the sky lights dance, but they are only good for hunting by. She does not look up at them and wonder about her place in it all.

She wakes in a place she did not walk to.
The smell of them is gone, the collar around her
neck is gone. There are flowers, bad for hiding in,
but there are animals too, she smells them in their
burrows. They are quick but stupid, and Fox is
quick and cunning. She waits by their burrows,
and snaps them up, one by one.

She eats her fill on the island, and lifts her nose to the wind. Ahead she smells birds, but they are across the ice. Fox knows she must be careful of ice. But there is another smell. Another fox. This and the birds mean there is not a choice. Fox checks the ice, low on her belly, and scents across the sea.

TWENTY

Leila fights her instinct to follow Mum, knowing she has no choice but to obey her instruction. Her heart is pounding harder than she can ever remember – except, she can remember. She remembers—

No.

Terror makes her feel heavy as a stone. Lying here hidden, something is rising to meet her, the past with long, spindly fingers reaching for her, threatening to drag her back. *I can't remember that*, she tells herself. *I can't remember.*

But of course she can. She remembers being packed between bodies in the dark, a blanket over her to keep the chill sea air away, thin plastic leaching cold beneath her.

Amma crying, Mona's cold hands wrapped around her.

Mum whispering – what was it? – about a dragon – yes, the water like a dragon.

Mona's teeth chattering as she asked for another story, and now Leila knows why she understood exactly what Mum meant when she said sometimes you need stories more than shelter or food, because that's what Mum did, she kept them warm and full of stories the whole journey to England.

She remembers it all. The night they left Damascus, bombs lighting the sky like fireworks. Basbousa, terrified in his basket, handed to their neighbour who would not leave. The car into the hills, a truck to the border. The smell of gasoline, the sound of crying, energy bars like sawdust in her throat. Amma chanting – *we are the lucky ones.*

She lets the remembering break over her like a wave. Walking awake, walking half-asleep, being carried, walking always in the dark. More cars, more trucks, a lorry where Mona had a panic attack and screamed silently into Amma's shoulder. A tent stoppered up with snow, snow pressing on the slack fabric, like an ogre stamping down on them as they shivered and waited for the boat. The boat . . . the boat.

The door opens, and Leila surfaces back to the present with a gasp, but it is Liv she hears, Liv who peels back the blanket. Her face is puffy, and she sits beside Leila. 'It's going to be all right,

Leila. But . . . your mum . . .'

'They took her,' says Leila, and her voice is calm though she is full of storms. 'The coastguard? She didn't have the right passport.'

'Yes,' says Liv, rubbing her eyes. 'I don't understand how they found out. Hans Island is half-owned by Canada. They knew she'd been there.'

And now the nausea Leila had fought rises, horror filling her veins.

'Me,' she says. 'It's my fault! I posted a photo— a photo of you all on the island. I put the location.'

Matty steps into the room, shaking his head. He crouches down next to Leila. 'I let you send that. I didn't even think, and I knew about the visa.'

But Leila is crying now, the shock fading and pain rushing in. 'It's my fault!'

'I am the adult here, Leila,' says Matty, and his voice is kind but firm. 'This is not your fault. And more than that, this should not have happened, no matter the photo. It is only because the military have fought over that land for years. We are Norwegian citizens. We have certain protections. But Professor Saleh—'

'She belongs just as much as anyone,' says Britt roughly. 'It isn't fair.'

'What will happen to her?' sobs Leila, forcing herself to look up.

'The coastguard has taken her to a detention centre on the mainland.'

Leila gives a small gasp. She remembers fluorescent lights, dirty toilets, cold showers and weeping women. Liv tightens her grasp on her hand.

'We weren't allowed to go with her,' says Matty, 'but there's a lawyer waiting for her. We'll make sure she gets out immediately.' His expression is furious, fierce. 'I promise you, Leila.'

They are all looking at her like she's going to burst into tears again. But instead Leila thinks back to Mum's determined face as she fought to save Miso from the ice, to her voice as she told a story about dragons from the sea. She would not leave it to lawyers. She had taken that photo, made this mess, and now she would work out how to fix it.

It is the longest time she's ever spent writing two hundred and eighty characters. Maybe the longest anyone has ever spent. She agonised over how to tell the story in so few words, and wrote it out a hundred times, but nothing feels urgent enough, serious enough, strong enough. In the end she decides the space needs to be used for the facts.

Dr Amani Saleh has been detained by the Canadian coastguard after freeing Miso on Hans Island. If you have followed Miso's journey and believe freedom matters, please support the woman who shared her with you. Tell the coastguard to #FreeProfessorSaleh #WhereIsMiso

She adds a photo of Mum, one where she is looking at the camera with her direct gaze, lipstick on, hair brushed.

She waits, refreshing, until the retweets start to rise. First one-by-one, then in multiples. People start replying to the tweet, asking if it's true, asking where to write to the coastguard. Some say horrible things, which Matty hides from Leila, and blocks the senders, but they are drowned out by the tide of worry from their followers, and then, as it gets spread beyond their circle, people who start to follow them. People quote tweet the message with hashtags – #WhereIsAmani – and slogans – No human being is illegal.

By the time Liv comes and insists it's time for bed, they have hundreds of responses and retweets. But the brief euphoria Leila feels fades when she asks Liv if there's any news, and Liv shakes her head.

Leila climbs into Mum's bunk, searching for her scent on the pillow, but she can't find it. Britt wriggles up beside her and even though Leila is squashed against the wall, she's glad. She wants Mona or Amma to tell her it's going to be all right. She wants it all to be a bad dream, and to wake up. She wants Mum.

She sleeps fitfully, waking up often and with a start, letting Britt stroke her hair until she falls asleep again. She dreams of foxes and dragons and pirates, islands splitting in two. When Liv shakes her awake, she thinks for a moment it is an earthquake, and she is stuck on the other side of a widening abyss.

She blinks blearily up at her mum's friend, who gestures for her to follow. Britt is fast asleep, an arm slung across her eyes. They slip out into the bright corridor.

'Mum?' says Leila hopefully. Liv shakes her head.

'Your aunt and cousin.'

'Where?' says Leila, looking around, her sleep-addled brain half expecting them to walk down the metal steps.

'On the satellite phone, in the map room.'

'They know?'

Liv grits her teeth. 'Everything.'

With a pit of dread in her stomach, Leila follows her down the corridor. Matty is sitting in front of the laptop, exactly as she'd left him. The shadows under his eyes confirm he hasn't slept.

He turns the screen to her as she sits down in front of the phone, and she sees the tweet has impossible numbers of replies and retweets and likes, and there are tabs open on everything from 'Canadian embassy' to 'Arctic Institute' to 'Detention laws for dummies'.

Liv puts her hand briefly on his shoulder, gesturing at the phone. 'We'll be just outside, OK?'

Leila picks up the phone like it might bite her. She can hear Mona and Amma arguing, their voices fading in and out like they're pacing the small sitting room. Leila swallows hard.

'Hi.'

Mona gives a small shriek, and there's a clatter as one of them knocks the phone off the table and picks it back up.

'Habibti, you're there? You're OK?'

'Yes Amma—'

'You're on a *boat*, Leila. A boat! In the Arctic Circle! What the he—'

'Mona, language.'

'She's in the Arctic Circle, Mama, I think it calls for—'

Hearing them bicker makes a lump swell in Leila's throat. She misses them so much her whole body aches.

'The *Arctic Circle*,' repeats Mona.

'I always was,' says Leila. 'Tromsø is in the Arctic Circle.'

'Are you being smart with me, Leila Saleh? When you get back from the Arctic Circle, I'm going to kill you.'

Despite herself, despite it all, Leila starts to laugh. 'How many times are you going to say it?'

'What,' says Mona. 'Arctic Circle?'

Leila hears Amma snort, and then burst into giggles.

'It's not funny, how are you laughing?' says Mona. Leila and Amma's laughter intensifies. 'Am I the only one who hasn't completely lost their mind?'

'Yes!' say Amma and Leila in unison, which makes them laugh harder. Mona mutters something about lunatics and the Arctic Circle, until finally the hysteria passes. Leila takes deep gulping breaths. It felt so good to laugh like that, like she hasn't since she left home.

'Now you've got that out your system,' says Mona frostily, 'can we talk about what's actually been going on the last month?'

'Liv said she told you.'

'I want to hear it from you.'

So Leila tells them, from the very start. About Fiona the flight chaperone, and the immigration officer, and Britt and Liv and Matty. About the bento box ('Eel? Ew.') and Miso and the funding. The boat and Captain Johansson and Lenny. About the cold, the ice, the bear (it was Amma's turn to swear), catching Miso and setting her free. About the coastguard, and finally, about remembering the crossing. When she mentions the dragon story, Mona lets out an audible sigh.

'I'd forgotten that.'

'I thought I had,' says Leila.

'Leila,' breathes Amma. 'You've been through so much. Why didn't you tell us?'

'She was protecting her mama,' says Mona. 'Weren't you?'

'Yeah,' admits Leila.

'But Leila, and don't take this the wrong way, because I love her. You know I do,' says Mona, 'But it's not your responsibility to protect your mama. She's the parent. That's what she's meant to do.'

'*Lillemor*,' says Leila suddenly. 'Little mother. It's a word they have here. It's what you are.'

'Insulting me now?'

'No,' says Leila, holding the phone tighter to her ear. 'I'm saying thank you, Mona. Thank you for looking after me, always. For protecting me.'

There's a long silence. Then Leila hears Amma murmur something, and Mona's voice comes through clearly, so Leila can tell she's taken her off speakerphone. 'Trying to make me cry now is it?'

'I love you, Mona.'

She hears a little gasp followed by a long pause and then Mona asks, in a voice that suddenly sounds younger and a little afraid, 'Are you coming back?'

'What?' Leila blinks at the phone.

'Mama made me promise not to ask, but I have to. It's fine, whatever you decide. But I just need to know.'

'Yes,' says Leila, and now she realises the feeling she had churning in her tummy when she thought about leaving Mum wasn't fear, but relief. She realises she loves Mum, but she loves Mona and Amma as well. That they are more than enough. 'Yeah. As soon as this is sorted out, as soon as I can. I'm coming home.'

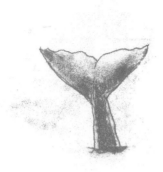

TWENTY-ONE

The news doesn't come for five days. Five days of tweeting, emailing anyone they can think of, speaking to journalists, and endless, endless waiting. Leila spends all her time below deck, drifting between the map room and the bunk room, between the online world and sleep. The only time she allows herself to be lured on deck is for whale sightings, more and more frequent but no less special for it. They see orcas on the hunt, clever and terrifying. They see sperm whales and more minke, and a whole pod of fin whales.

But the one that grips right on to Leila's heart and squeezes, is seeing a blue whale. This time she spots it: a massive, barnacled back, a spurt of water. So close Leila could take a running leap on to its back, could cling on and be borne to the deepest part of the seas. And then the tail, forked and scarred, pushing up out of the water, splashing down with a force that sends the boat swaying, coating them all in spray.

They whoop and cheer as the whale dives, and Leila, tired and scared and sad as she is, feels again that emotion she felt seeing Miso for the first time. The thing she didn't want to call love, but which had no other name. Not just for the whale, but for this family she's found on the boat, in this wild place. For this landscape Mum left her for, and brought her to. For the whole glittering, freezing, fearful and wonderful world she'd never known existed.

Leila is trying to sleep in her bunk when the door swings open.

'They're flying her to Svalbard!' says Liv, 'Your mum will be there tomorrow morning.'

Liv shows Leila the map she's clutching. 'We'll be a few hours behind her, that's all.'

'You've spoken to her?' Leila is trembling. 'Is she OK?'

'I haven't, but her lawyer confirmed she'll be on the plane tonight. She says the pressure you put on the situation sped everything up hugely. You got her home, Leila.'

Liv hugs her and Leila feels her body crumble. She is too

drained to even cry. But one feeling breaks through: hunger. Her stomach rumbles loudly, and Liv laughs.

'Come on. You're coming up on deck for breakfast. No arguing.'

Leila eats like a starved thing, the stale bread and salted fish like the most delicious thing she's ever tasted. All her senses feel alive again.

Captain Johansson comes to sit beside Leila. 'I am so glad it is ending like this,' he says. 'I hope you know I did my best for your mother.'

'I know,' says Leila, realising that everyone has been blaming themselves. Matty, Captain Johansson, Liv, Leila herself. But really none of them were at fault. Even Mum did nothing wrong. Even the coastguard was following the rules.

This is something that has come to Leila slowly and as a great shock. That the rules are wrong. That it was rules like that which meant they had to leave their country illegally and travel so dangerously. Rules that drew lines and made Lenny have to leave his family to become a fisherman. All these things, designed to keep them apart and out of places, to make them feel like they didn't belong.

Miso had shown what could be done if you crossed those lines, but when Mum had done it, she'd been taken from them. She knew Mum was lucky, that thousands more people were trapped or locked out of where they needed to be. Leila didn't know how to fix that, but bringing Mum home was a beginning.

.

They reach Longyearbyen on Svalbard exactly twenty-four hours later. It is a strange, beautiful place, made stranger by the fact there is an airport and a town in the middle of a place so remote. Leila thinks back to arriving in Tromsø, and how quickly her ideas about the world changed, how its centre shifted.

They will meet Mum at the airport and fly straight back to Tromsø, which means more goodbyes.

'Thank you,' she says to Captain Johansson, who already has another charter scheduled for the following day. 'I hope your future lady scientists aren't as much trouble.'

He laughs. 'That would make life very boring indeed.'

Lenny gives her a tight hug. 'Bye Leila.'

'Bye, Lenny. Maybe see you soon.'

'Maybe,' he says. 'But it's all right if not – I'll remember you, and Britt.'

'I'll remember you too,' grins Leila. 'I'm glad we met.'

Standing on the dock feels as weird as standing on the boat had that first time. To not have snow or ice or sea below her – only concrete.

*

The drive to the airport is so short they can see the terminal from the dock, but it feels like an age. Finally, the car is pulling up in the car park, and Leila goes spilling out of the door before Matty even cuts the engine, running like she's never run before, towards the beautiful, brown skinned, tired-eyed woman standing in the brisk wind, her arms wide open.

Mum smells of unfamiliar soap and toothpaste. She feels thinner. But when they finally break apart, she is smiling wider than Leila has ever seen, wider even than when they'd seen Miso for the first time.

'La-La,' she breathes. 'I swear you've got taller.'

'Maybe you've got smaller.'

Mum laughs, a real, full-throated laugh. 'Detention centre food is no bento box.'

'Worse than the boat?'

'Maybe not that bad.'

Leila knows they're speaking like this, being silly, because they aren't ready to talk about it all yet. But it's OK, because for the first time with Mum, Leila feels like they have time.

Liv comes screeching across the tarmac, Matty and Britt close behind, and envelops Mum in the tightest hug Leila's ever witnessed. She could swear Mum's eyeballs bulge.

'Amani, you wonderful, stupid woman! I could kill you!'

'Please don't,' gasps Mum. 'The amount of paperwork I've

had to fill out, I can't imagine what it would be like for murder.'

They FaceTime Amma and Mona, all of them crying until Matty sidles into view in the background of the call. Mona snaps to attention like a wolf on the hunt, wiping her cheeks.

'Who is that total smokeshow in the glasses?'

Leila wrinkles her nose and makes a *yuck* sound. 'Matty?'

'Hotty more like,' says Mona, preening. 'How's my makeup?'

'He's far too old for you,' says Mum sternly. 'And he's gay.'

Mona sighs. 'There's always a catch.'

Matty blushes, and Leila guesses he heard or guessed their conversation. She waves him forward.

'Hi.'

'*Hei. Hvordan har du det?*' says Mona in perfect Norwegian. 'What?' she grins. 'TikTok does language lessons too, y'know.'

'You are full of surprises,' says Mum.

'Says you.'

Relief pools in Leila's stomach to hear them all joking together. She nuzzles closer into Mum's side, and as they say their goodbyes, she feels a dizzying sense of happiness.

Their flight leaves three hours later.

'Two planes in a day,' remarks the airport officer. 'I've never known such excitement.' He is so friendly Leila forgets to be nervous and smiles with all her teeth.

They are the only passengers on the plane, which is small and has propellers. When they take off, the island becoming map-sized below them, Leila's ears pop. She digs in her pocket and finds the very last Werther's Original.

She sucks it until the pressure in her ears fades. Mum is asleep beside her, head lolling, and Leila thinks about the other mothers she read about on Twitter, still separated from their children. She rests her head on Mum's shoulder and promises not to take a single moment for granted, grateful that when they part it will be her choice, however hard it is to make.

They touch down only an hour and a half after taking off, the grey buildings and mountains of Tromsø oddly familiar. It is definitely summer now, the snow on the mountains melted, and bursts of yellow gorse visible even from the great height. It makes Leila think of Miso on her flower-strewn hillside, snapping at insects.

Standing at the conveyer belt waiting to collect their bags, Leila feels like her head might spin off. It's like Britt said, like being in a different time as well as a different place. She doesn't know how people move between worlds like this. But she has a feeling she wants to find out.

TWENTY-TWO

The restaurant is every bit as crowded as it was the first time, but the two of them squeeze on to a narrow bench, knees bumping, and raise their soups to Miso, and to being together.

Leila thinks about the question she has been waiting to ask. *Why did you leave me?* But she's scared. So much has happened and so much has changed. The lines of their relationship have shifted and all that matters is being here with Mum. But, as if she's read her mind, Mum starts to talk.

'It's okay—'

'Please,' says Mum, reaching across the table and squeezing

Leila's hand. 'Let me say this. I've been practising in my head all day.'

Leila waits as Mum gathers herself, takes a breath.

'I know I've not been a good mum, a good sister, a good aunty. In truth, I've never felt like I fitted in any of those categories very well. Even at home . . .' She takes a sip of jasmine tea. 'It felt wrong, somehow.'

Leila feels a pit open in her stomach.

'But when I became *your* mum, Leila, I couldn't believe my luck.' Mum looks directly at her, and Leila feels her cheeks flush. 'You are the best thing that ever happened to me. And fleeing home – that was the worst. All of us uprooted.' Leila feels the heat of Mum's gaze, of all the emotion coursing through her. She's been holding it all back, just like Leila has, and it seems to be just as painful for her. 'But while Amma seemed relieved to be in England, I realised it wasn't the right place for me. I know that makes me selfish, but I didn't feel safe there,' says Mum, and Leila can almost feel her desperation to be understood coming off her in waves. 'I saw you and Amma and Mona, and you were this unit, this perfect happy unit, and I could see only one way to add to that. By working at the institute, I could bring in more money. I could make your life better.'

'But you don't get paid loads,' says Leila. 'I've seen your flat, remember?'

Mum smiles sadly. 'Why do you think I live in a shared flat like that?'

Leila frowns, and then it dawns on her. Mum is the most important person on her team, so she must get paid the most. She lives like that because she sends all her money back to them. To her. The hairs lift on Leila's arms. All this time, she's misunderstood. Mum took this job so they could live in their terraced house in Croydon, and have new trainers, and always have enough food. Leila doesn't understand how she never realised before, how she never thought where the money came from.

'I didn't leave because of you,' says Mum a little desperately. 'I left *for* you. To provide for you, as well as for myself. I felt like I had no purpose. In Damascus, I had my work, but in England no one would employ me. I knew you would be happy with Amma and Mona.'

Leila's instinct is to argue, but she can't. She can't lie. The truth was, she had wanted Mum there, but *need*? Mona and Amma had given her everything she needed. All the love, the support, the protection. By the simple fact of leaving, Mum had shown she couldn't give Leila what she needed. And even though that hurt, it also made sense.

'Why here?' says Leila finally. 'Why Tromsø?'

Mum seems to think hard about her answer. 'You know I've always loved telling stories about faraway places, unimaginable landscapes, even dragons,' she smiles at Leila. 'When I saw that

I was allowed into this country, when I found the opening at the Arctic Institute, it was like the pieces aligned. This strange place where it is light and then dark for so long, a place where dragons are said to have lived. It felt meant. I know this is hurtful. I hope you know I would give it all up for you.'

Leila feels the world turn as she hears those words, the words she's longed to hear, to know her mum understands how hard it has been for Leila without her. She knows her mum is telling the truth, she believes her with every fibre of her being.

'I don't want you to give it up,' she says, squeezing her mum's hand back. 'I want you to keep going. Look at how many people love Miso, because you did. How many people care that she has somewhere safe to live. You're changing people's minds.' Leila feels her cheeks flush. 'You changed mine.'

Mum smiles. 'You understand so much, my La-La. What Miso did, why she did it . . . it's incredible, yes, but it's also a warning. We had to leave our home, because of war. But what if it was because of water, or lack of it? Or the weather? Patterns are changing. Miso's journey proves that migration is necessary for survival. What Miso did, what we did, was leave home to find something better.'

Leila nods. 'Do you think she did?'

'What?'

'Find something better?'

Mum draws her closer into her side. 'I think so.'

'I think so too.'

Leila leans against her mum's shoulder. 'You're not like most mums, but you're mine.' She thinks of Britt, talking about how her family arrangement was different, but it works. Leila had her mum, her amma and her *lillemor*. More love than most people could ever dream of. 'I am happy, but if we could do this, get together, even once a year, it would make me the happiest person in the world.'

'More than once a year,' says Mum. 'As soon as it's confirmed the Norwegians aren't kicking me out, I'll book to come see you for the Christmas holidays when you and Mona are both off. If that's all right with you?'

Leila feels a bubble of warmth growing inside her, and for that moment she has a clear, shining vision: that everything will be OK.

After dinner they walk by the quayside, looking at the light-blue haze hovering over the sea. It's nearing midnight, and everything feels hushed and paused.

'Are you tired?' says Mum.

'Not especially.'

'Good,' Mum smiles and links her arm with Leila's. 'We'll get there just in time.'

The walk across the bridge is longer than expected. Ahead,

the cathedral rises like an iceberg, lit with a soft golden light. Now they are closer, Leila can see ribs of the rafters through the triangular window, similarly lit to gold.

'We're going to the cathedral concert?' Mum nods. 'But you have to book.'

'I know,' says Mum, pulling out a piece of paper from her coat pocket. 'I did.'

They are among the last to enter the hushed warmth of the cathedral. As they walk through the large, heavy door, the atmosphere changes, like a blanket of snow. Leila's skin tingles. A choir and organist are already assembled at the front. Leila and Mum settle themselves in the backmost pew, just as the music starts.

The triangular windows over the altar are filled with stained glass. The blue of it reminds Leila of Miso's fur, of thick ice, and a whale's tail disappearing into the sea. As the singing starts, it hits Leila right in the chest. It seems to shine gold in the air, like breath made visible. She doesn't really care about hymns, or classical music, but there is something about hearing it here, with her mum beside her, that fills her heart.

She promises herself she will come back, maybe in the winter, when the Northern Lights dance in the sky. But until then, until she can sit on this hard pew and listen to people singing a language she doesn't understand, she will carry it with her, this feeling. This feeling that she belongs.

Winter, and Fox's mate has grown white as the snow. Fox stays blue as the rocks she was born among. The land here is different, so she is different, mimicking her mate's movements, matching him stride for stride on paws grown fluffy as her tail.

They wait in the long dark days together, listening for lemmings below the passages of ice. Soon there will be cubs to feed, puffins to hunt. Their bodies keep each other warm. They do not go near easy meat.

The scientists are showing her to the world. Miso, they say, walked all this way. They show the miles, on the largest maps they have.

But miles mean nothing to Fox. She knows only that she has come, to exactly where she is meant to be.

ACKNOWLEDGEMENTS

Thank you to our families and friends for their constant love, support and inspiration. Thanks especially to the Furnivalls for posing in the cold.

Thank you to the Hachette Kids team: to Rachel and Nazima for Leila; to Alison for Fox; to Emily, Naomi, Valentina, Sarah, Ruth and everyone working to bring them to readers around the world.

Thank you to Hellie for her guidance and encouragement.

Thank you to Sarah for the donation to CLIC Sargent (Young Lives vs Cancer) that meant your niece Leila Potter's name inspired the girl in our book. Thank you Leila for letting us borrow it!

Thank you to Peter for photographing hundreds of paintings and drawings.

Thank you to Inclusive Minds and to Jasmine Nilsson, whose rigorous and brilliant reading made this book so much better.

Thank you to booksellers, teachers and librarians for helping children find our stories.

Thank you to you, for reading this book and making its world come to life.

Thank you to each other, for all we are building together.

FURTHER READING

See booktrust.org.uk/booklists/ for brilliant recommendations by theme. Here are some of our favourite books on these topics.

ON MIGRATION

The Crossing – Manjeet Mann (12+)

Illegal – Eoin Colfer, Andrew Donkin and Giovanni Rigano (10+)

The Arrival – Shaun Tan (8+)

My Name is Not Refugee – Kate Milner (6+)

Boy, Everywhere – A.M. Dassu (9+)

ON ANIMALS

The White Fox – Jackie Morris (8+)

The Last Wild – Piers Torday (9+)

The Girl Who Stole an Elephant – Nizrana Farook (8+)

Twitch – M.G. Leonard (8+)

October, October – Katya Balen (9+)

AUTHORS' NOTE

Miso's journey, as incredible as it is, is based on a real crossing made by an Arctic fox; the scientists who tracked her called her Anna. Anna walked over 2,000 miles in 76 days, making it the longest and fastest fox migration ever recorded.

She really did travel from Svalbard, north of mainland Norway, all the way across the Arctic to Ellesmere Island, in Canada. She used sea ice and glaciers, just like in our book. Her story was recorded by two scientists: Eva Fuglei (Norwegian Polar Institute, Fram Centre, Tromsø, Norway) and Arnaud Tarroux (Department of Arctic Ecology, Norwegian Institute for Nature Research, Fram Centre, Tromsø, Norway). You can read their paper online – it's very interesting! As always, real life is just as amazing as the stories you can read in books. We need to look after our world and its animals, and keep telling their tales.

Leila's story is also based on real-life migrations, specifically of children fleeing war in Syria to try to find safety in the UK. Too often, our governments ensure it's nearly impossible for people to enter our country safely, and some UK citizens believe that is the right thing to do. We believe this is driven by a misplaced fear, prejudice, or ignorance about refugee people and migrants.

Migration has always been part of the human story, as it is for every animal. Kiran is the granddaughter of migrants, as are many authors, nurses, actors, doctors, politicians, refuse collectors, teachers, lawyers, shop assistants, and all sorts of people who make the UK their home. We should welcome them.

But just like Leila finds out in the book, many more of us need to raise our voices and fight for people's right to live where they choose. Being born in a peaceful country is only a matter of luck – no one is better than anyone else because of where they are born.

Kiran Millwood Hargrave and Tom de Freston
Oxford, May 2022

Kiran Millwood Hargrave and Tom de Freston met in 2009,
when Kiran was a student and Tom was artist-in-residence at
Cambridge University. They have been a couple and collaborators ever
since, but *Julia and the Shark* was their first novel. It was Indie Book
of the Month, Scottish Booktrust Book of the Month, and won the
Waterstones Children's Gift of the Year 2021.
Kiran is the award-winning, bestselling author of stories including
The Girl of Ink & Stars and *The Deathless Girls*, and Tom worked as
an acclaimed artist for many years, making his illustrative debut with
Julia and the Shark, and his writing debut with *Wreck* (Granta, 2022).
They live in Oxford with their cats Luna and Marly,
in a house between a river and a forest.